A Grave Matter in Hampton Pogmore

David Penn

Bonker Books

www.BonkerBooks.com

Synopsis

Henry has had enough of the disagreements, arguments and friction between him and his wife, Hannah. Henry is too old to start again, and has to much to loose, unable to deal with her heavy demands any longer, he plans to do away with her. Alone in the pub, Henry has some weird and wacky thoughts as to how she will vanish. Catching one of his many idea's, he suddenly has it. A plan in position, he goes home to commit the perfect crime, well, nearly perfect…!

Contents

Chapter 1

The last straw

Which of the final straws that finally committed Henry Pilkington to murdering his wife was never clear to him. He had toyed with the idea for years, allowing his imagination to conjure up her slaughter in the most unspeakable ways from struggling, suffocation to total dismemberment depending on the degree of hatred he felt at the time. Perhaps it had been his statement from the Bank, torn open and carefully scrutinized before he had a chance to see it for himself. The cold impersonal figures revealed even more excessive spending by, Hannah than usual and that was excessive enough.

In his capacity as chief clerk, he needed to be careful as overzealous spending was frowned upon, overdrawn situations intolerable. At this rate he was likely to be suspected of fiddling the books. Such a mistake opening a joint account. Hannah adopted the belief that she was in a joint account with the Bank itself. Perhaps it was her intolerable probing of his mind, never satisfied until every detail of his working day was revealed, vindictively critical of any variation which took place. Henry had felt mentally naked for twenty years. Perhaps it was her excessive tidiness. Everything from newspapers to neckties would be banished from sight before Henry could take breath. He was almost scared to sit down and disturb the pristine condition of the cushions. In all probability it was her latest decision to spend a few days with her mother. Not that such a visit was unreasonable, but a few days every month was when Henry was left to fend for himself, shop and feed himself and cope with the chores. He was well able to do so, but, on her return, every detail would be examined, laying bare his every move, spitefully itemizing everything he had not done. Her departure was welcomed, but her return reduced Henry to a nervous wreck. In fact it was none of those things that finally tipped the scale. It was the May Bank Holiday weekend. Henry had a few days off and the weather was unseasonably warm, with clear blue skies and temperatures above 22 degrees. He decided to soak up some sunshine. Winter in the confines of the Bank had sapped his reserves. He rooted about in the shed and found a deck chair, after a struggle he placed it on the lawn facing the sun and settled down with a book he had been trying to read for a month. It was only fifteen minutes before Hannah appeared with a clothes horse. She plonked it on the path and glared at Henry.

"What do you think you're doing? You get time off from your precious Bank and sit on your backside. The shed needs painting, so does the fence and instead of sitting on the lawn you could be mowing it."

"I need some sunshine, stuck in the Bank all day is depressing. There's plenty of time for other things."

Hannah snorted and disappeared into the kitchen, returning after a few minutes with a basket full of washing. She set about hanging a load of underwear on the clothes horse. She disappeared again. Henry went back to his book. After a short time the sun went out. Startled, Henry looked up at the sky. No clouds and then he realized. Hannah was hanging sheets and a duvet cover on the clothes line, blotting out the sun completely and leaving Henry totally in the shade.

"What the Hell are you doing?" he shouted. "You've blotted out the sun."

Hannah smiled, maliciously, "Perhaps that'll

get you off your backside."

It was enough, Henry got up and stalked off, grabbed his jacket and left the house. The local pub the, Goose and Duckling, was ten minutes away. As he walked he cooled down, his anger subsided and a strange thing happened. His hatred of Hannah resolved from an ongoing bitter resentment into a cold and resolute determination. He would kill the bitch. He had thought of leaving her and making a clean cut. Leave the wretched woman to her finicky world of tidiness and greed. But where would he go? His work would be in ruins, his career ended. At 51 years of age he would be as employable as a clothes brush in a nudist colony. Besides she would bleed him financially dry… she had almost achieved that anyway. He reached the pub, bought a pint of bitter and settled himself in the beer garden. He began to think straight now that the decision had been made.

How would he do it? Stick a knife into her cold heart? Too much blood! Poison?... Take to long! Shoot her, he hadn't got a gun, and had no idea how to get one. Strangle her! That appealed to him, the thought of his hands around her scrawny neck cheered him up, he bought another pint.

Chapter 2

Mundane Marriage

He returned home fortified by a couple of pints. Hannah sneered at him.

"More money down the drain, or rather into the barman's pocket. You're the one who moans about spending money, different when it's on you!"

Henry said nothing. Coming to a sudden end your bitching he thought. The prospect gave him a warm glow.

"Another thing I can't understand why you object to me visiting poor mother. She isn't well, been very lonely since daddy died. I have a duty to her as her only daughter. Besides you don't miss me, all you think about is your damned work."

"Dammit she's as strong as a horse you only

saw her a fortnight ago. Duty? What about your duty to me. I earn all the money you spend. I can't do my work properly if I have to do your work as well."

"Duty to you?" Hannah sneered, "You don't appreciate me, you never have you wouldn't notice if I dropped dead!"

Henry glared into her face. Well let's find out he thought. 'Let's bloody well find out. His mind was made up he was going to somehow murder her as brutally as possible as soon as he could. The Pilkington house sat solidly at the top of Acacia Drive, commanding a fine view of the whole village. It was a corner house, built by a local builder in the immediate post war years. A large fenced front garden ceased abruptly at the integral double garage and resumed the encirclement of the house at the rear. The Garage had been largely commandeered by Hannah to house her white Fiesta, a large chest freezer and a plumbed in washing machine. In a corner there were carefully stacked tea chests filled with unneeded pots and pans and bric-a-brac collected over the years, and which had no place in the scheme of things within the house. Such items would make the cupboards untidy and the thought of steam hazing the windows from the weekly wash, was intolerable. Hannah had banished the washing machine to the garage from day one, much to Henry's annoyance there was little room left for the mower and garden tools, and certainly no room for his ageing, Ford Cortina which was exposed to the weather all year long.

The weather was a problem in Hampton Pogmore. The village nestled snugly in a deep valley in the heart of unspoiled Warwickshire and was protected from the biting winds of winter, but suffered from heavy snow drifting and was completely cut off on occasions for weeks at a time. Mr. and Mrs. Hawkesbury, owners of the village general store, come post office, home made pie shop and bakery were enterprising folk and did very nicely thank you in the winter. The total population small though it may be, were compelled to buy locally during the icy months. Outside transport found it too dangerous to attempt the steep and winding only road into, Hampton Pogmore leave alone the hazardous attempts to climb out again. The shop never ran short. Heavy stocks were intentionally laid in during the autumn and prices rose mysteriously with the first frosts.

Herbie Andrews, Landlord of the Goose and Duckling, also did very well in winter. Ensuring that a roaring log fire burned day and night, the pub was a welcoming place for those unfortunates, who either made no provision for heating oil, nor were able to obtain any once the roads were icy. Most properties were centrally heated with oil fired systems, gas was impossible in the remote village. For a tanker to venture down the hill after December 1st was unheard of. There were stories of one brave soul who attempted the descent only to become wedged across the High Street until well after Christmas, having first leaked four thousand gallons of Shell oil into the already inadequate drainage system. The village stunk of oil fuel for weeks and generated the catch phrase of the year, "You can be sure of Shell."

As the local Police Constable was the only representative of the law, and was himself no mean drinker, Herbie never suffered the embarrassment of the restrictions of the licensing laws. The Goose and Duckling was used as a communal meeting place, and somewhere to keep warm and sales boomed. However, winter had passed and it was Spring in Hampton Pogmore. The hillsides glowed with primroses and wild daffodils and the village hummed with activity, and the inevitable motor mowers, and at weekends the dedicated made preparations for the annual entry to the, "Britain in Bloom," competition. Twice the village had pulled off first prize over the last ten years and would have won the previous year but for Bert Smithfield's hungry sheep. A gate, left open, allowed them to stray into Market Square during the early hours before the judges arrived. They had munched happily on the roses which decorated the island outside the Council Offices. Bert who was also the local butcher had noticed a distinct lack of interest in the sale of lamb for a long time afterwards.

The Vicar of the Church of St. Augustus, the reverend, Timothy Smallfoot was also a keen contributor to the floral arrangements for the competition. The small church clung precariously to the hillside some distance back from the road into the village. It was surrounded by the overgrown graves of many past generations and the available space for new arrivals edged nearer and nearer to the slowly crumbling walls of the Church. It was a matter of grave consternation to the Reverend Smallfoot. He was a dedicated Minister and had been the Vicar of the Parish for more years than he cared to remember and he viewed with concern the gradual deterioration of the ancient Norman building. As each new applicant for permanent occupation reduced the space between Church and graveyard he was sorely tempted to start again at the outer periphery. But he was sure there were descendants of the long crumbled bones who would create a furore should he do so. Instead he compromised and instructed, Fred Perkins to plant flowers and shrubs along the roadside edge of the burial area feeling sure it would meet with approval. In the Autumn he could then strip the flower beds and use it for future clients without criticism. So nice to be planted with the flowers he reasoned. Fred, the local gravedigger, handyman and general Church factotum set to with a will and developed a 5ft. wide strip alongside the low wall. Plants and flowers were plentiful donated, willingly by the villagers following a moving sermon delivered on mothering Sunday. As Easter approached Hampton Pogmore settled happily into the routine of comfortable co-existence and would, no doubt, have sailed smoothly onward into the balmy Summer except for two, totally unrelated happenings.

The first was a profound decision by a pimply faced youth in the District Council Offices, that the main road was in dire need of repair, due to damage caused by ice and severe frosts during the past winter. The timing was of such repair work, was as usual, completely thoughtless.

Hampton Pogmore benefited from the stream of visitors, many from overseas, who drove aimlessly through the village during the Easter break gazing with glazed eyes at the quaintness of an English village. All aspects of the village commerce benefited, from the sale of ice-creams, cream teas, to meat pies and sweets, not to mention pints of flowers bitter and the opportunity for the Vicar to coerce them into donating to his appeal for £10,000 to help restore the Churches foundations. The prospect of having the only road churned into dust and savaged by bulldozers throughout the profitable season caused an uproar. As is normal their complaints made no difference at all and the date was fixed. The second unfortunate circumstance related to Patrick Murphy, who became a father for the fifth time late in the afternoon a couple of weeks after Easter. He celebrated his great achievement not wisely but too well in the public bar of the, Goose and Duckling, until late into the night. But for these commonplace occurrences, Henry Pilkington may well have faced a different future than that which was ordained.

Chapter 3

Alone and Able

Henry had returned to an empty house rather earlier than was normal. He usually left the Bank at 5pm sharp. Today he had made the excuse of feeling unwell, and had busied himself in a large electronic equipment store in Coventry. Hannah had left for her mother soon after, Henry had departed in a very bad temper that morning. Her mother lived a mere 30 miles distant and she felt quite competent to drive that far. In any event, Henry had refused to take a day off and drive her. Henry cared not. Hannah was a dreadful driver but she ought to know the road like her own toothbrush by now. The House was spick and span as usual nothing out of place. A note, written in a hurried scrawl, sat arrogantly on the cooker.

'Food in the Fridge.' Make sure you clean up

properly make the bed, water the primulas….only once.'

Henry scowled at the potted primulas which sat on a cork mat on the kitchen windowsill. He screwed up the note viciously. He made a cup of tea and unpacked his purchases. A small cassette recorder, two tapes, a tiny microphone and a press button switch. He also had 10 metres of transparent lead. Now that he had decided to do away with Hannah, he was going to do it properly. He didn't relish the idea of 15 years behind bars, although, if the Judge knew Hannah, he might be able to plead justifiable homicide.

Two hours later, Henry pressed the switch and began talking to himself. He found no difficulty in finding what to say. He was eloquent and expressive in his feelings toward Hannah, outlining her faults and his hatred of her. Switching off he groped behind the refrigerator and extracted the cassette. He slotted the tape into the music centre which graced the lounge. He rewound the tape and pressed play. His own voice spoke to him. It sounded weird and loud, he turned the volume down enjoying the disembodied confirmation of his own feelings. It was as though he had an ally who thought the same as he did. He rewound the tape and wiped it clean. Henry was well pleased the recording was clear and precise...although his voice sounded different. He then replaced the recorder behind the refrigerator, secreted the wires amongst the leads already leading from the socket. Hannah was terrified of electricity she certainly wouldn't be poking around in that area. The microphone was hidden behind the wall clock and the switch taped beneath breakfast bar near the supports, even she wouldn't spot that.

Hannah returned after a five day absence and life resumed the normal pattern. Easter was now only just over two weeks ahead, falling in late

April this year. Henry was never quite sure how they fixed Easter. It seemed to vary each year that passed. Probably determined by the Meteorological Office who picked the wettest weekend and plumped for that. Whatever it was, Henry was banking on Easter to provide the opportunity for his next move. Aggravatingly Hannah was less spiteful and critical than normal, even subtle remarks by Henry aimed at getting her going had little effect. It was not until the Wednesday before Good Friday that the opportunity presented itself. Henry was munching toast at the breakfast table.

"I *must* go to see mother for Easter."

Henry pressed the switch and continued eating. "Pardon?"

"I said I was going to see mother for Easter."

"You've only just come home from seeing her for Gods sake, I've got four days off over the

Easter Holiday, possibly including Tuesday as well. What do you think I'm going to do with myself? I thought we might go away somewhere to get a break." Henry spoke louder than usual, but with disappointment in his voice. "I really don't know why you don't live there permanently and just pop up here occasionally."

Hannah bridled, resenting the objections, She launched into a tirade of abuse. Henry fed her the ammunition and she fired on all cylinders. The impartial tape revolved silently behind the fridge imprinting Hannah´s voice indelibly on its' surface. Frustratingly, Hannah comprised. She grudgingly delayed her departure until the morning of Easter Sunday, emphasizing that she had considered him as much as he deserved. Henry watched the Fiesta disappear with impatience. Once the car had disappeared he collected the tape and dismantled the recorder, then he sat down with the music centre and his editing equipment. It took him four hours. Tired but jubilant he listened to the edited tape. It was perfect. All that remained was to dispose of the gear. Under the cover of finishing the trench for his runner beans, and careful to avoid the eyes of the prying neighbours the cassette and other aids were securely buried. Henry went to bed. Henry took advantage of the Easter break to mix with the local inhabitants. He lunched at the Goose and Duckling, allowing himself to wallow in the sympathy which followed the disclosure that, Hannah had again left him to fend for himself. Henry was well liked. Most of it was tempered by the knowledge that his word decided whether or not a loan, mortgage, or overdraft would be approved, but much was due to the belief that a man just can't cope on his own, whereas a woman could be depended upon to manage even in the most dire circumstances.

Gordon and Mary Moore, Henry's next door

neighbours, invited him to dinner. Henry accepted, aware that the reason was to learn as much gossip as possible... Mary was the village busybody, able to turn any snippet into forbidden fruit, even the prospect of being plagued by the Moore's three children did not deter him, the Moore's were important to his plan. Mary listened avidly as, Henry discussed Hannah over the roast beef. It wasn't that Hannah had no feelings for him, he was quite willing to understand why she was concerned for her mother. It was just that life was so empty without her. Mary tut-tutted with sympathy. Hannah was lucky to have such an understanding husband she thought, obviously she didn't think so much of Henry as he believed... lucky not to get a damned good hiding running off at the drop of a hat. Sounded as though she might leave him for good, wouldn't take much!

Henry slept well, full of copious helpings of

home-made apple pie, his dreams filled with a glorious future where everyone loved him and did all they could to please him. Two weeks after Easter the opportunity, Henry had been waiting for presented itself, whereupon he very nearly changed his mind. It was all very well to plan things and fantasise over the result, but when it came to actually carrying out the deed, waves of fear flowed through his body. Hannah had been home and reasonably content for almost three weeks. It was the right time. It was Sunday evening and Hannah was avidly watching the television, "only time she shuts up," thought, Henry "watching these soap operas!" He turned the pages of the local paper to the section dealing with the affairs of the village. *It was there*…The one entry he had been waiting for and dreading.

"On 29th April, suddenly at Pogmore Cottage, the passing of Maud Elizabeth Hodge, aged 89 years beloved of the Parish and mother of, Sarah and Percival. Funeral Service and burial at St. Francis Church on Tuesday 4th May at 3pm.

Henry's heart thumped. So old mother Hodge had gone. Hadn't done too bad, she was after all 89. Burial on Tuesday, just right.

"Are you alright?" Hannah's voice startled Henry. He jumped and dropped the paper. "You've gone pale, are you ill?"

"Certainly not!" Henry recovered. "I'm perfectly OK." He coughed to clear his throat. It felt dry.

"Probably getting another cold... puzzles me why you don't take care of yourself more. I wouldn't worry, but you pass these things on, you know how ill I am with a cold, you might be more considerate."

Henry said nothing. "Be bloody cold where you're going." He thought. He got up and went to the bathroom. Locking the door he sat on the

25

seat to compose himself. Was he really prepared for this. It was such a drastic step. No going back once he'd fixed her. Had to be sure. The vision of Hannah´s curled lips filled his mind. He was sure, damned right he was sure. It had been planned so carefully. He ran over the details, it would work. It would have to work. Anyway without a body they couldn't prove anything, just circumstantial evidence. They could assume all they liked, all he had to do was to make sure everyone knew where he was at the time. All the time *they* thought anyway. Henry stood up and flushed the toilet. He took a deep breath. It was 9pm. Hannah was watching a comedy on Channel 4. Always watched what she wanted, never asked, just flicked the programmes about as it suited her. She sat with her back to the lounge door her greying hair above the easy chair. Steeling himself, Henry walked towards her the cord from his dressing gown looped in front of him. With a sudden surge of desperation that surprised himself, he looped the cord around Hannah's neck and dragged it tight. The shocked Hannah was able to emit a short gasp before the cord cut off her breathing. She struggled wildly rising from the chair, clutching frantically at the cord with both hands. Henry pulled and tugged as the chair toppled backwards. Hannah came with it, slithering across the floor towed by a frantic Henry. Her legs thrashed wildly and her body writhed against the onslaught. With panic, Henry looped more cord around the thrashing head and dragged at it as though he wanted to sever it from her body.

"Die you bitch...for Christ' sake die!" He blasphemed gasping for air himself.

After what seemed hours Hannah's body slumped, deprived of oxygen her struggle stopped. Henry kept the cord tight, closing his eyes in horror at what he had done. He kept tension on the cord for a long time, frightened to let go, frightened she may recover and leap at him. Finally he let go, and her inert body slumped to the floor. He rushed into the bathroom and was violently sick. An hour later, white faced and still shaking, he ventured back into the lounge. Hannah lay where he had dropped her. Her eyes bulged and her mouth seemed blue...like a blue gash where the swollen tongue had been thrust in from the outside, rather than protruding from within. Her face was waxen. Shakily he felt her macerated throat. The skin was torn and bloody where the cord had bitten into the flesh. There was no pulse. He pressed his ear against her chest. There was no heart beat. Hannah was dead. Henry was violently sick again. Much later he drank the remains of a half bottle of brandy. It made him feel no better. It was done, God forgive him it was done. Now he must pull himself together. No good unless he carried out the rest of the plan. Amazingly he found he was crying.

Chapter 4

The perfect Place

From the spare bedroom Henry collected the under-blanket from the bed and carefully remade the bed, just as Hannah would have done. He knew what he had to do and carried out the procedure almost automatically, he had practised it in his mind often enough. He wrapped her body carefully in the blanket, and, with a ball of heavy string lashed it into the shape of a naval hammock making sure the ends were secure. There was no blood. Thank God for that, he didn't think he could have coped with that. Hannah was heavy, very heavy it took all of Henry's strength to drag her to the connecting door of the garage. The Fiesta stood quietly, resentful, as he dragged and rolled the body to the front of the washing machine. Once there, it resembled just another addition to the cluttered and packaged possessions. Henry closed the door and sank wearily into the armchair. He wished he had some more brandy. Later, after working on the Fiesta for an hour Henry Pilkington went to bed. He didn't sleep a wink!

Early the next morning he busied himself in the kitchen making the normal noises. The Moore's were up and about, their children making enough racket to wake the dead. He regretted the simile. Their windows were open to the bright sunlight. He followed suit, opening the lounge window as wide as possible. He slotted the tape into the music centre turned up the volume and played the tape. His heart was pounding.

"I must go to see mother." Hannah's voice vibrated from the speakers. Henry felt ill. The earlier recorded conversation carefully edited, continued, seemingly taking place there and then. References which would have dated it had been erased. The relevant remarks engineered originally by Henry added to another, apparent disagreement between, husband and wife. It was possible to sense the eavesdropping by the Moore's and almost feel them listening. Henry felt a bit light-headed as the tape came to an end but he continued to talk to himself giving an apparent, grudging acceptance of the apparent trip. Gordon Moore left for work soon after 8.30 am. Henry waited a few moments and left himself as he would normally do. He parked his car in a small side turning and waited. Just before 9am. Mary Moore drove by on her school run, as soon as she was passed, Henry returned home on foot. Calling as little attention to himself as possible he drove away in Hannah's Fiesta.

In Coventry he parked the car in the multi-storey car park, on the third floor. The car park was widely used, the Fiesta would not be noticed, not for a long time. Rubbing a duster around the steering wheel and the door handles he locked the door and threw away the parking ticket. The interior had been stripped of any personal items and he had changed the number plates for a pair he stole from an abandoned, Fiesta ditched outside a breakers yard. He left by the iron staircase and returned home by bus, collecting his car on the way. He arrived at the Goose and Duckling just as lunch was being served. Although he wasn't really hungry he forced a home-made steak and kidney pie down whilst informing the landlord, with due sadness, that, Hannah had left again on one of her trips to mother. The landlord was duly sympathetic and bought, Henry a pint.

The reverend Smallfoot was delighted, his Church was more than half filled, an unusual occurrence, competing as he did on Sundays with the licensing hours of the Goose and Duckling. Such a pity that the occasion was one of such solemnity. However, one could not hope for everything. Maud Elizabeth Hodge had contributed to the Church more in her passing than she had in her many years of life. Her coffin stood in solitary splendour, covered in the flowers of Spring, midway along the aisle. The Reverend coughed (he always coughed to command attention) not that there was the same need today, everyone was quite respectful and subdued. He spoke of the sincerity of Maud's good works in the village, of her kindness and dedication to all her friends and neighbours, her virtues and courage for accepting the loneliness of widowhood on the passing of her husband years before. He did not mention the reason for her husbands passing, enough to remember that sales of Whisky dropped significantly after he was laid to rest. He spoke with enthusiasm, an enthusiasm he didn't really feel of life in the hereafter.

"It is not the end...just the beginning." The congregation looked suitably impressed.

Maud was carried reverently to her last resting place which had been carefully prepared by the dutiful Fred Perkins. The grave lay as close to the footpath as was possible and had caused some dispute between, Fred and the Vicar.

"Much, much too close to the Church Fred." Intoned the Reverend.

"Better than stacking em in the back pews Vicar, there's no more room out there, less you wants em put together...no telling what they'd get up to."

In the face of such blasphemy the Vicar capitulated and stalked off. Maud Elizabeth duly rested next to the footpath, the Vicar intoning the burial service pressed uncomfortably against the flaking walls of the Church. Henry, who had not attended the funeral, later walked through the churchyard after the mourners had departed viewing with casual interest the mound of soft soil heaped on the grave. The soil was loose and would be allowed to settle for a few days before, Fred tamped it down. By that time, Maud would have a companion chuckled Henry, who was fast regaining his confidence and sense of well being. He had always believed that the most obvious was inevitably the least obvious. Where better to hide a body than with other bodies. Other murderers, he quailed at his newly acquired title, left bodies in obvious places. He had found the ideal hiding place. Like hiding an apple in a cider mill.

Chapter 5

The Deed is Done

Henry was fully dressed in his oldest clothes. To retain possession of these had been quite an achievement. They had been banished to the garage after his stints in the garden, or cleaning the car. This time there would be no need to stow them away in the corner, they would be burned. He had everything planned. He lay fearful of dozing off on the settee. For the first time he could remember he was unconcerned about ruffling the covers or resting his feet on the pouting arms. The television had long since finished, although he had no idea of which programmes had flickered across the screen because his concentration was elsewhere. If he was seen tonight that would be it, very much *it.* He looked at his watch for the twentieth time, the damn thing hardly moved. At last it was 2 am. He rose to his feet. Now that the time had come he felt fear, more fear than he had ever felt before, including the act of choking the life out of Hannah at that time the adrenalin had helped. Now his guts were as heavy as lead, the corners of his mouth trembled with tension. There was no going back, he couldn't leave the bloody woman in the garage trussed up like a roll of lino. The Cortina was backed into the garage, boot lid raised. Henry cursed the designer who left a raised rim along the rear end of the boot, why couldn't the floor be level with the edge. He heaved Hannah across the sill and dumped her into the space he had prepared. The spare wheel lay in the garage to make enough room. God she was heavy. Henry stood still to recover. Slamming the lid he cautiously opened the garage up and over door. He smiled with self satisfaction at his foresight in oiling the springs, the door rose quietly. He started the engine, quailing at the horrendous noise the starter motor made in the confined space and drove slowly away without lights into the dark streets. There were two entrances to the Churchyard. One curved across the front of the old Vicarage and wound across the front of the Church. He didn't take this risk, no telling if the Vicar was was up having a late prayer session or a glass of milk, maybe something stronger. The old boy was no angel, not yet anyway. Henry giggled a little hysterically. The other was, in fact the exit and was well out of sight from the gaunt, and darkened house. Besides it, was just inside there that, Fred kept his tools of trade. Spades, shovels, pickaxe and wheelbarrows were stowed in a rather dilapidated shed which leaned sadly against an immense yew tree. Fred always locked it, not realizing that the tongue of the lock failed to connect with the twisted jamb and, therefore, was totally useless.

The car turned slowly into the driveway, crunching the gravel, past the shed and into a turning area reserved for the hearses to park during the burial services. The Vicar parked his dark green Metro there, Henry stopped alongside the little car. Two cars were less conspicuous than one on this occasion he reasoned. Henry climbed out and listened. The moon was playing hide and seek with a flurry of dark clouds, appearing and disappearing every few minutes, There was no sound, no sign of life, not that you'd expect it in this place thought, Henry. The shed door opened easily and, Henry carefully lifted a shovel. Walking on the grass verge he made for the grave of, Maud Elizabeth. It was, as he had last seen it, still soft and covered with wreathes and flowers. The Church loomed above him, casting a black shadow across the pathway and the grave. Even the fragmentary appearance of the moon failed to relieve the shadow. All was well. He began to lay aside the wreathes and flowers, careful to remember how they had been placed, and began to dig away the soft earth, pausing every few minutes to to listen and look around. It took about fifteen minutes of digging to prepare a shallow trench deep enough to contain Hannah but not to expose her body if, Fred was a bit energetic with his final preparation of the grave. Leaning the shovel against a nearby gravestone he walked back quickly to the shed. The wheelbarrow stood on end at the back of the hut, it moved easily on a worn and half inflated tyre. Cautiously, Henry pushed it, praying it would not squeak, it didn't it grunted. Hannah's body was draped half across the barrow and Henry struggled to push the unwieldy load across the spongy grass. It was hard work and he toyed with the idea of hoisting her on to his shoulder, but the thought made him shudder. She had probably started to decompose by now. He broke out in a cold sweat.

At last he reached the grave and thankfully rolled Hannah into it. She lay about 9 inches below the surface level. Breathing a sigh of relief, Henry in a bit of a panic now, began shovelling earth back on top of the blanketed corpse taking care to cover the whole length of the grave. He didn't know which way she faced, not that it mattered. The replacement of the wreathes and flowers took time but at length he looked at it and was satisfied, he put the shovel in the barrow and took them back to the shed. Henry sat in his car, his heart pounding in his ears. He waited and watched, ears tuned to catch the slightest sound. There was nothing. He had done it, thank God he had done it. It occurred to him that to thank God, especially where he was for helping in a murder was hardly the thing to do. He drove slowly home and into the garage. He stripped off his old clothes and stuffed them in the incinerator at the foot of the garden. He would burn them tomorrow. More tired than he remembered being all his life he crawled into bed after a very large Scotch. Spasmodic nightmares, followed by a hazy unconsciousness, left him at 8am looking as though he had more right to be in a grave than the two unfortunate women. He lay in a bath hoping to soak away the trauma of the previous night. He was late for work.

Chapter 6

Speculations

"You really don't look well at all Henry." Mary Moore peered at him across the garden fence. "You look tired out you poor soul. You ought to have a holiday, somewhere in the sun, sit about and eat nice things."

Henry smiled his woebegone smile. "I haven't really recovered from the food poisoning Mary. Must have made a mess of cooking my own food. I think it was the chicken. Hannah says you must be careful with chickens they can bite back."

"What food poisoning?" Mary looked shocked. "I didn't know...when was that?"

"Soon after Hannah left me alone again." Henry pulled a face full of suffering." I really find it difficult to look after myself properly. I thought I would roast a chicken. I get so tired of fish and chips and easy food. I tried but I must have done something wrong. I was very ill for a day or two, I went to work but I wasn't really well enough."

Mary set her lips, "I know it isn't any of my business."

Whether it was any of her business or not she was going to have her say. "Hannah has no right, no right at all to leave you alone the way she does. I think it's cruel. A woman should look after her husband first, even before the children, that's what we are for to cherish and feed amongst other things. After all your husband is your life… where would the family be without him. He has to be fed and cared for! Not left alone whenever the mood takes her. I've a good mind to give Hannah a piece of my mind."

Henry smiled wanly, "You're very kind, Mary. I hope she'll come home soon, it's been ten days now."

Mary snorted, "When is she coming home?"

Henry shrugged, "I don't really know... she never tells me until the day before. It seems to depend on how her mother is...you know how women feel about their mother."

"No I don't, I love my mother but I don't intend to race off to see her and leave Gordon high and dry. Poor dear would pine away."

"I love Hannah too," murmured Henry. Mary sniffed loudly.

"I think I will ring her and ask her to come home. I really don't feel well enough to keep the house as she likes to have it." Henry smiled bravely.

"You do that Henry. You just do that, and you will come to dinner tonight." Mary raised her hand in rebuke as Henry started to protest. "I won't have no for an answer, if someone doesn't look after you, Hannah will come home to a

46

corpse."

"That'll make two of us." Grinned Henry to himself. He was careful to maintain the expression of a puppy who had been offered a table scrap after all. Henry did ring Hannah´s mother.

"Can I have a word with Hannah please." Henry was coldly polite, he had never had any time for his mother in law, any more than she had for him.

"Hannah is not here Henry. I haven't seen her since Easter, as you full well know."

"Cow!" thought Henry.

"Don't be silly she has been there for ten days, as you know. I want to speak with her."

"Have you been drinking?" He could almost hear the expression of disgust.

"No I damned well haven't …I want to speak

with my wife. Now put her on please and stop messing me about."

"I repeat, Hannah is not here. I haven't seen or heard from her since she went back to you." There was a note of resentment almost as though returning to Henry was an act of desertion.

"Listen," Henry introduced a note of exasperation into his voice." Hannah left here ten days ago to spend even more time with you. She didn't even have the courtesy to let me know she had arrived, nor did you. I've been struggling to manage on my own, and, now I need her to come home, where she damned well should be. Will you please put her on the phone."

"Henry, Hannah is not here." The voice sounded anxious now. "I promise you I have not seen her, not since Easter. If this is some sort of joke please don't worry me. I am not a well woman."

Bloody sight fitter than you deserve to be thought Henry. Pity he hadn't planned things a bit better he could have knocked the old bag off as well. He pulled himself together.

"If you insist. Just tell her to get her backside back here as soon as possible. I'm not prepared to put up with her long visits to you any longer." He hung up.

Henry waited. Within two minutes the phone rang. He grinned and let the phone ring six times. As he expected it was Hannah's mother, anxious and worried about Hannah. Was Henry joking? Where could she be? Had Henry told the police? Henry led her on until he finally accepted that there was need for concern. He promised to ring the Police. Over dinner he related the facts to, Mary and Gordon.

"I can't understand it," he muttered, savouring the Yorkshire pudding." She didn't even get to her mother... where could she be? She couldn't have left me. We had our differences, who doesn't? But we loved each-other, no need to run away."

"Of course." Placated Gordon. "Nothing has happened I'm sure she has probably gone to stay with friends. Perhaps she felt she needed a break."

Mary glowered at him. Tactful as a sledgehammer was Gordon.

She leaned towards Henry consolingly. "I think you ought to tell the Police, you do hear of such awful things happening these days, murder, muggings, rape even."

Henry choked over his sprouts, she should be so lucky, "he thought." I will tell the police, but I'm sure she is OK, she does get these funny turns, imagines the world is against her, that no-one cares. All I have ever wanted to do is make her happy." He spared time from the last roast potato to look sincere.

Later he rang the Police, duly sympathetic they recorded the details. They contacted Hannah's mother who was immediately frantic with fear and voluble with her condemnation of Henry who was an inconsiderate husband. There had been no reports of an accident, no reason to suspect foul play. Hannah was duly entered in the register of missing persons and a description circulated of her white Fiesta. Henry spread the word of Hannah's unjustified disappearance throughout the village and the clientèle of the, Goose and Duckling considered the implications, and finally came out in favour of what had happened.

"Good riddance I say."

"Henry ain't going to miss er, she was never 'ere."

"Poor old sod he'll be better off in the long run."

"Wish my old woman would bugger off."

"Can't be another fancy man, less he's broken out of the, 'Funny Farm!"

The feelings ran in Henry's favour and for a few days he was assured of a pint or two until the novelty wore off and the subject dropped in favour of slating the Council for destroying the peace and tranquillity of Hampton Pogmore, and the inability to drive out of the village without the risk of a shattered windscreen. Patrick Murphy was just about to start his voyage of destruction tearing up the cracked surface of the main road.

Chapter 7

By Pure Chance

The first day of the Council's activity, was, in fact typically inactive. At 7am. a small white van disgorged two men in yellow coats, who spent the next two hours studiously drawing peculiar signs and numbers on the approach road. They walked through the village, hands clasped behind their backs puffing acrid smelling pipes and talking earnestly in low tones. Coincidentally they disappeared at 11.30am. just as Herbie Andrews unbolted the doors to the Goose and Duckling and weren't seen again that day. The next morning was a very different matter.

Patrick Murphy, a robust and ginger haired Irishman from Dingle Bay on the West coast of Ireland, set dogs howling and chickens clucking in panic as he clattered and grunted a huge and rusting Bulldozer into position at the top of the hill. Patrick loved his bulldozer, he gloried in the power and destructive force the machine delivered and was happy when he was tearing down buildings and ripping road surfaces to bits. He sang continuously in a bellowing, off key voice which was thankfully drowned in the dreadful racket that the bulldozer created. Today he would totally destroy the narrow footpath which wound, single sided into the village. There were a number of houses which needed access across the footpath. These had been marked out by the men in yellow coats. He had been instructed to keep these clear for entry, but, apart from that he had clear rein. New levels were to be set. Curbstones inserted and drains renewed before the top surface of the road could be laid. Patrick began to sing as he ploughed his way into the footpath. The telephone in the Council Office rang continuously, the villagers complaining about everything, from disrupted television to

Doctors Surgeries, terrified old ladies and paranoid animals. One even complained about Patrick singing. This, upset him as he had a high opinion of his vocal talents. Dead on 5.30pm an uneasy peace descended upon Hampton Pogmore. As if by magic the dozer ceased its clattering, and workmen disappeared as if all one man. The night was fraught with misgivings as to the next day when it would all start again.

It took, Patrick only four days to pulverize the pathway and he returned the bulldozer to the top of the hill on Friday afternoon preparatory to commencing further destruction on Monday morning. As he broke for lunch, which he took regularly (mainly liquid) in the, Goose and Duckling he received the joyous news. Mrs. Murphy had given birth, earlier that day to a fine bouncing, Patrick junior. Weighing in at nearly 11 pounds after a short labour, he increased the, Murphy family to seven in all. Patrick received the news via the telephone in the pub and immediately increased his liquid intake buying beer all round and treating everyone to a heart rendering version of *"I will take you home Kathleen."* Mrs Murphy was blessed with the name of Kathleen, which was very appropriate. By 3pm. Patrick was out for the count and snoring loudly, draped across the window seat. Herbie didn't have the heart to throw him out, beside when he sobered up no doubt he would be off again. Patrick slept on. At six he roused bleary eyed and hungry. The other workmen had gone home also the worse for wear, so, Patrick imparted his joyous news to the new arrivals in the pub as he munched his way through four of Mrs. Hawkesbury's meat pies. Enjoying a new audience to share in his great achievement, Patrick celebrated for a second time that day, until, by 11 pm, he was again as drunk as an owl and just as starry eyed. This time, Herbie had no compunction about heaving the staggering Irishman out. With encouraging words, Herbie suggested that he had better go home to see his new member of the family, or at least to recover enough to see him the next morning. Being reminded that the next day was Saturday cheered the befuddled, Patrick enough to set him on his homeward journey. He staggered past the recumbent bulldozer and smiled affectionately. It sat malevolently by the roadside, the huge shovel poised in the air like a gigantic admonishing hand.

"Are yer alright me darlin, keeping yerself as quiet as ye can I hope. Oil be after setting yer goin again soon." He clambered up into the drivers cabin and patted the controls. "Behave yerself now... don't go looking at any of them fancy tractors."

He stood up and swayed towards the edge, his head swimming with the exertion of climbing into the cab. Suddenly he lost his footing and stumbled across the uneven plate floor grabbing at anything he could to save falling five feet to the ground. His hand grabbed the first gear shift which, being well worn slid out of gear, another grab released the already defective brake. Patrick was so unsteady that he didn't feel the first lurching movement of the machine. So used to lurching himself he stepped out into space and crumbled in a heap at the side of the monster as it started to move. Patrick was sick, the sudden tumble had been too much. He crouched by the mangled roadside groaning with nausea, not noticing the grinding rumble as the bulldozed gathered speed. Even in his distressed condition he couldn't avoid the shock at the noise, and, the fact that the dozer was on its way downhill, faster and faster as it went.

He leaped to his feet, "Holy mother of God," he screamed, "Me bulldozer....me beautiful bulldozer. Stop you bloody tin can."

Patrick set off in hot pursuit until he trod in one of the ditches he had created earlier and spread his length in the rubble. His ginger head struck a chunk of paving stone and Patrick Murphy knew no more.

The bulldozer, uncaring, ploughed its unstoppable way down the steep hill, the shovel flapping up and down with every bump and careering from side to side of the uneven road. The noise was deafening, worse than if the engine had been running, and lights sprang from windows as the digger thundered past. At the bend in the road, the bulldozer, mischief in its heart, stopped swinging from side to side and set its sights on the sharp bend which was racing to meet it. Now on a straight course it aimed itself like a huge cannonball and increased speed until it finally smashed through the low wall of the graveyard churning up the flowers so carefully planted by Fred Perkins.

Undeterred the monster ploughed on, flinging mildewed gravestones hither and thither as if they were made of cardboard. One hardy headstone, bearing the effigy of an Angel in full flight, collided with the flapping shovel and slammed it into the down position, whilst the Angel did indeed take flight and collapsed in a mound of powdered masonry fifty feet away. The shovel, now locked into its most destructive position, scoured and dragged a deep trench across the graveyard as the tons of machinery hurtled forward. Finally with a screech, it ripped across the pathway and embedded itself in the wall of the Church. With one final 'clank' it came to rest, the shovel slowly lifting, and regaining its aloft position. Terrified by the noise the Reverend Smallfoot hastily donned a moth-eaten dressing gown. He burst out of the Vicarage, scared to find the cause of the pandemonium. He stopped, aghast as he saw the huge digger embedded in to the wall of his Church. In the pale moonlight the ravages of the graveyard showed clearly. The lower strata of the Church wall was almost demolished. Even as he stood, speechless, another ancient brick toppled to the ground. He looked skywards in a panic, the whole Church could topple, the Reverend had the utmost confidence in God but he moved swiftly out of the danger area. God moved in mysterious ways. The Reverend wasn't taking any chances.

Chapter 8

Palpitations

Within half an hour the population of the village was aware of the catastrophe. The Fire Brigade and Police had arrived in force, as had 60 plus people from the village. Someone had discovered the intoxicated Patrick, deep in the ditch at the top of the hill and assumed he had been run over by the bulldozer. That being so, the ambulance driver had stated, "He has to be dead and we don't take dead bodies. Call the Police van."

Further frantic examination of the Irishman disclosed that clouds of best bitter were emitting from his blue lips. He was dead alright, dead drunk. The driver loaded him into the Ambulance. The Chief Fire Officer decided that the Church was an unsafe structure.

"Sorry Vicar," he smiled apologetically. Not going to be able to do much sermonising this Sunday. The righteous will have to have a day off."

Sergeant Winterfield agreed. "The whole Churchyard will have to be sealed off, too dangerous, kids you know, little blighters always creep around anything dangerous. Doubt whether we'll raise the Council before Monday. You know what they are, they all emigrate on Friday afternoons. Best to leave things until Monday. I'll put a P.C. on 24 hour cover. Reckon this is going to cost a few quid by the look of it, cost a fortune to restore the Church, and the graveyard. Look at it, like a bloody bomb had dropped. The Insurance Company won't be very happy."

The Sergeant gazed around the disaster area.

The Fire Officer grinned. "They'll say it was an act of God."

The Reverend Smallfoot glowered at him. So it was that all was left as it stood, or nearly stood, late on the Friday night. The occurrence provided a talking point for the clientèle of the, Goose and Duckling for weeks to come and, by early Saturday there was no-one who hadn't heard of the runaway bulldozer. No one that is except Henry Pilkington, who slept soundly and trouble free throughout the excitement of the night. It fell, inevitably, to Mary Moore to impart the latest item of gossip to Henry. As he ambled into the garden on Sunday morning she leaned over the fence in her most confidential manner. Henry knew something, or someone was about to be destructively discussed.

"Morning Mary," he smiled wanly.

"Morning Henry...you'll have heard of course?" Mary always liked to determine whether she was first off the mark, or not.

"Heard what?" Henry wasn't very interested.

There was enough examination of peoples private affairs on the television if he needed that sort of thing.

"The Church... almost demolished by the blessed Council. I knew there would be a disaster using those great machines. In my day a few hard working men with shovels would have done the job just as well."

Henry looked at her quickly. "The Church?" What was up with the Church. He had a special interest there.

"Demolished."

"What do you mean demolished? you're joking Mary!"

"Well," breathed, Mary, *"Almost demolished.* One of those awful bulldozer things ran amok and slammed into the Church after tearing up the graveyard. All those gravestones smashed and the flowers ruined! No chance of winning the contest now."

Henry was really worried now. The graveyard ripped up. Christ Almighty if, Maud's grave was one of the graves Hannah could be sitting up in full view. He went white.

Mary looked at him, startled in the change. "The contest is not *that* important Henry... you mustn't get so upset...we can soon plant some more flowers." She looked at Henry's' ashen face with concern.

"Damn the bloody contest," he snarled, "How much damage was done?"

Mary was quite shocked. "There's no need to blaspheme like that... on a Sunday too. Whatever has upset you. The bulldozer ran down the hill and smashed through the wall. It ripped up a lot of ground, and, has damaged the Church wall, that's all. No need for you to take on so. The Fire Brigade won't let anyone in, it's too dangerous."

Henry pulled himself together, mustn't give himself away. Not to Mary of all people. He summoned back his self control.

"I was thinking of the Vicar." He muttered lamely. "The poor man has all his time cut out trying to repair the Church as it is."

Mary smiled again. "There now how like you to worry about other people, the Vicar will be alright. The council will have to foot the bill, and, he'll finish up better than he ever was. Just you see... trouble is the rates will go up to pay for it."

Henry excused himself and hurried indoors. His mind was in a turmoil. If the grave had been damaged, you can bet it would be the one with Hannah in it, had to be. Sod's Law would see to that! Opening the garage door he drove towards the Church, desperately trying to to form in his mind a direct line from the rise of the hill to the Church. He couldn't. Setting his lips he prepared himself for the worst as he swung into the entrance. The gate was firmly closed. A large notice proclaimed, 'DANGER NO ADMITTANCE. UNSAFE STRUCTURE. It was signed in felt tipped pen by Sergeant Winterfield.

Henry climbed out of the car and walked across to the gate. He could see the huge bulldozer fast against the Church wall with the shovel raised high in the air above the buckled cabin, but the path it had taken was obscured by an ancient row of yew trees along the edge of the wall. He hurried to the next entrance. As he walked along the crumbling wall he searched the area desperately trying to place Hannah's last resting place. At least what he had hoped would be her last. Could very well be the first of many he groaned. Half way along he stopped dead in his tracks. There was no doubt about it. The huge shovel had scooped a path directly across three graves and the last was, Hannah's. He could see the mashed wreathes and flowers scattered in all directions. Where the raised mound had stood, nothing remained but a gaping trench. He strained to see how deep the trench was, it was too far away, but it seemed to be just as deep as it was before he dropped Hannah into it. Henry felt sick of all the bloody luck, fucking great graveyard like that and the fucking thing had to gallop across the one grave that mattered. Henry felt entitled to swear. All his careful planning gone down the chute. He toyed with the idea of climbing the gate and carrying out a closer inspection, but decided against it. That would really call attention to himself. Perhaps if he called upon the Vicar... with condolences, an offer to help. Henry winced, the only help the Vicar understood was a handful of banknotes, however, any sacrifice was worth it.

He hurried to the phone kiosk on the corner. There was no phone book, only a crude drawing of the male genitalia with a phone number to ring if you wanted to see the object in the flesh. Henry snorted and dialled Directory Enquiry. He waited and waited until at last a sleepy voice asked what he wanted. The Vicarage telephone number was forthcoming. Henry dialled. The Vicar would be pleased to see him. Mr Pilkington must stay by the gate and await the Vicar, to be guided around the danger area.

Once ensconced in the Vicars study Henry expressed his concerns, so negligent of the Council, what a blessing no-one was killed. However would the Vicar cope without a Church and the sacrilege of disturbing those at rest.

"Does it mean there would have to be re-burials?" asked Henry, "Recompense to the relatives for the damaged headstones?"

The Vicar pressed the fingers of his hands together and smiled sympathetically.

"It is very touching Mr. Pilkington that you

should have taken the trouble to call with such sincere feelings, especially as it is rare that I see you normally."

"Nasty, that," thought Henry, he smiled sheepishly.

"Fortunately," the Vicar went on, "there appears to be no desecration of those laid to rest. This bull thing only really damaged the surface, some 12 or 18 inches deep."

"Quite bloody deep enough," Henry thought.

"Our Fred Perkins ensures that the departed are deeply plant – buried, there is no need for a re-burial."

"What about double graves Vicar?" Mused Henry absently.

"Even they, dear Mr. Pilkington, we ensure that the last arrival enjoys the full depth allotted to them. You seem very interested? Have you a dear one in such a resting place?"

Henry shook his head. Better shut up the old boy was getting suspicious.

"Not at all Vicar, it just seemed to me that the Council will have to find the money to repair the damage and, Fred Perkins will be put to a lot of extra work as I can't see the Council repairing the damaged graves. Perhaps a small financial gesture would ease his burden, he has worked so hard for the beautiful gardens contest."

Henry took out his wallet and slid out a ten pound note. The Vicar looked impressed, but not impressed enough. Henry slid out a second tenner.

"How extremely generous," The Vicar beamed and took the money without hesitation. "Perhaps you would like to see the ravages of the modern machine? We must be careful not to venture into the danger area but, at least you will be able to see what, Fred will have to contend with."

This was exactly what Henry had been angling for. He accompanied the Reverend eagerly as they set off. Skirting the pathway and giving the Church a wide berth he looked earnestly at the trail of damage tutting from time to time. As they reached a point where Hannah's grave was visible Henry moved nearer.

"Please Mr. Pilkington, no nearer. It really isn't safe you know."

Henry moved back, but not before his worst fears had been realized. The grave had been gouged out like a spoonful from a thick blancmange, quite deep enough to have shovelled Hannah out and cast her blanket and all into full view. Frantically trying to control the panic in his guts, Henry flicked his eyes in all directions. There was no sign of the blanketed bundle. No trace of anything except mud and debris. Hannah had disappeared. He hardly heard the voice of the Vicar coaxing him back to the gate. He took his leave with a heavy heart and even agreed to become a regular to the Church when all was back to normal. As he drove home it was almost a lost fragment of his life. What the Hell had happened to the bloody woman! She couldn't have decomposed in a week or so. Besides the blanket would still survive. Did Fred put lime in the graves? Had she been eaten by a ravenous pack of foxes. He shook his head, he was getting hysterical. Of course, the answer was obvious. The bulldozer had squashed her deeper into the grave, instead of scooping her up it had flattened her deeper, nearer to, Maud. Henry breathed again. Thank God she hadn't been left in full view of Sergeant Winterfield.

Chapter 9

Not Just a Silly Job

Life resumed its normal pattern for, Henry. As the days passed, and there was no ominous knock on the door. He became convinced that his speculation had been correct and that Hannah, had indeed been thrust deeper into the grave by the Bulldozers headlong rush. Casual inspection as he passed the Church showed that, Fred Perkins had tidied up the graves and that, Maud Hodges grave with its extra tenant, had been one of the first to be renovated. The Council workmen had erected scaffolding across the damaged front of the Church and the offending Bulldozer had long since departed, no doubt to wreak havoc on another unsuspecting village until it was time for the final onslaught on Hampton Lucy. Henry couldn't believe his luck, this had really sewn up the whole affair, as far as he knew the search for Hannah, if it had ever been seriously undertaken, had cooled. No doubt the County Constabulary had many more important matters to attend to than bother about errant wives buggering off. Life was sweet for Henry. He received tender loving care from Mary Moore, who, did dinner for him twice a week, and Sunday lunch with the Moore family became a regular routine. Henry reciprocated by bringing gifts for the children whom he despised really, but was happy to put on a happy face in the light of the comfort he was offered. His work became more interesting, and he amazed his seniors by the cheerful manner in which he arrived, and busied himself. The customers were also impressed by his joviality and it generally accepted that grass widowhood totally agreed with Henry Pilkington.

One Thursday, Henry opened the door of his office for a 3pm appointment. He blinked. It was

Fred Perkins. As far as, Henry was concerned, Fred was not a client of the Bank, or any other Bank for that matter. He had seen the name, Perkins in his diary but not associated it with Fred. Puzzled, he ushered a clean and smart, Fred to a chair. Possibly come to thank him for the twenty quid, mused Henry although he had never really believed the Vicar would pass it on.

"This is a pleasure," he greeted Fred, "What brings you to the Bank... come into a fortune?"

"Ahh... could say that." Fred sounded quite mysterious. Henry frowned and felt a draught of disquiet. Although the Hannah business had been pushed to the back of his mind, any association with the graveyard still gave a twinge. "Thought I might get meself a loan Mr. Pilkington."

Fred settled himself comfortably in the chair. Henry noticed he had put on his best, and probably only, suit and that his hair was washed and brushed close to his head. Henry had never seen Fred except when he was in overalls and normally smothered in mud.

"I don't believe you are a customer of the Bank Fred? We normally reserve loans for our own clients."

"These ain't normal times."

"Oh?" Henry looked at him strangely. "What do you need the money for?"

"Ahh! all lots of things, good things, like clothes and holidays. Food and booze... them sort of things."

Henry laughed, "Don't we all Fred, but I'm afraid we don't make *loans for them sort of things.*" He parodied Freds accent.

"'Bout time you started then, ain't it?" Fred was very calm and serious and Henry felt a tremor of fear. "Course if you was to make me a gift instead, that's up to you... I just thought it would be easier to get the money through the

Bank, they've got plenty ain't they?"

Henry's mouth dropped open. Fred may be a labourer but he had never struck him as a complete idiot. Obviously you can never tell. He decided to humour Fred.

"Really, you must be joking. The money in the Bank belongs to all the people who bank with us. It isn't yours or mine. We act as trustees if you like, investing and…"

"So invest some in me," interrupted Fred. "Got to be the best investment you'll ever make Mr. Bloody Pilkington."

This time there was no missing the underlying threat in Perkins voice. Henry's stomach clenched and he stared at the little man who sat so confidently across the desk.

"It's like this. Mrs. Pilkington was never one of my favourite people. Always had a nasty comment about the state of the graves. Never a nice word. I don't blame you for knocking her off."

Henry nearly fell off his chair with shock. "What the bloody Hell are you talking about, Perkins," he spluttered. "How dare you!"

Fred grinned. "Found er I did... little while ago now, all wrapped up snug in er blanket. Ad a good look, no doubt about it... Mrs Pilkington. I says to meself, someone ain't done you no good. Not with them strangle marks around yer neck, not with being trussed up like a Christmas Goose and not with being moved in with old, Ma Hodge. Poor old duck... ain't got much say in the matter ave she?" He grinned at the shaking Henry.

Henry struggled to contain the nausea which welled up in his throat. With a tremendous effort he looked Perkins in the face and controlled his twitching mouth.

"Don't you worry none Mr. Pilkington... your

secret is safe with me. Long as I gets me loan. You understand?"

Taking a deep breath Henry fixed Fred with a hard look.

"You say you found my wife? Where? You bloody little liar. Where did you find her?"

"In the scoop... scoop of the bulldozer. There she was, stuck up in the air like the Statue of Liberty's relief, happy as Larry. Been scooped out of the grave like a pip from a lemon. Thought she was an old carpet I did, til I looks closer... gave me quite a shock I can tell you."

Henry sagged in his chair. So that was what had happened to Hannah. Stuck up in the air in the bulldozer scoop. Nearest she'll ever get to Heaven he thought maliciously.

There was, however no doubt about it, Fred knew the whole story, he was done for. No wonder he was after a loan. Blackmail that's what it was. Creepy little shit. He would have no part of this, he would get the swine behind bars, somehow, but how? He would implicate himself. Henry capitulated.

"What is it you want Fred, assuming what you are rambling about is true... which it isn't."

"Now you're talking sense, just a loan, £5,000 or so... I've never ad £5,000 in my life."

Even in his misery Henry was puzzled, a loan... not a gift, just a loan.

"And how, may I ask are you going to pay back £5,000."

"I ain't... you are. I gets the £5,000, and you pays it back, over a year, by putting it into my account."

"Are you mad, it would cost over £500 a month to pay that back in a year."

Fred nodded. "That's right... then we starts

again, another £5,000 unless inflation pushes it up a bit. That way I'm in the clear. I applies for a loan and you approves it, case you was thinking I was blackmailing you. Wouldn't do that, nasty business Blackmail."

"And if I refuse?" Henry was livid, "I'll break your fucking neck first."

"Now now! don't make a habit of this murdering business. I shall tell Sergeant Winterfield about the lady in the blanket."

"Where is my wife now?"

"Back with Maud Hodge. I planted er again. Snug she is away from prying eyes."

Henry felt sick. "And if I were foolish enough to pay you."

Fred put his finger to his lips. "Shan't say a word… not a sound shall pass my lips."

"By the time the first year has passed there'll

be nothing left of her you fool." Snarled Henry."

"Cept er ead… funny things eads, they stay there for ever, and teeth… they can tell a lot from teeth."

"Hannah had false teeth."

"Did ave."

"What do you mean, did have?"

"I've got em now." Fred patted his pocket.

Chapter 10

Nipped in The Bud

Henry was drunk, very drunk, he had bought a bottle of whisky on his way home and had drunk most of it on an empty stomach. He felt light-headed and stupid, but the tragic sequence of events still penetrated his dulled thinking. He had to silence, Perkins... have to kill him, that's all. There was no other way. If the bloody swine was allowed to talk, then he was done for. They only had to dig Hannah up for the umpteenth time and there would be no escape.

But he *couldn't* kill him... he wasn't a murderer. Killing, Hannah had been different somehow, besides how would he get rid of another body. He couldn't go through all that again... unless it was made to look like an accident. How did a Gravedigger have an accident? Fall in a grave and break his bloody neck? Perkins didn't drive a car, never seemed to go outside the Churchyard except on his bike. Henry's mind rambled on through a haphazard series of actions until he passed out on the settee and sank into oblivion. His whisky induced sleep was haunted with nightmares of being chased around tombstones by an infuriated roll of carpet.

The morning found Henry with a size ten hangover and an appearance like the Angel of Death. He phoned the Bank and placed himself sick. Whether the terrifying nightmares had anything to do with it, or the cups of coffee he poured down his throat, he didn't care, but, amazingly his mind was clear. A solution had appeared in his throbbing brain. He thought about it, sipping yet another cup of scalding black coffee and began to cheer up. It would work, it had to work, he would be free of Perkins. Free from Hannah and free of the whole damned business. That afternoon he went to the Police. He asked to see the Detective Sergeant on duty and was ultimately shown into an upstairs office.

Sergeant Collins was a conscientious officer who was seriously overworked. He set himself a list of priorities. Top of the list were cases, which, if solved, would bring him recognition, and ultimate promotion. Second on his list were cases which received scant attention and were passed on to underlings, until something turned up which had promise of a clear up. Then, Collins took over. He badly wanted to be an Inspector. The case of Henry Pilkington and his lost wife interested Collins not at all. Impatiently he ushered Henry to a hard chair which had suffered the removal of two inches from the legs. This left the seat on a lower level than the seat behind the desk, and, in the opinion of Collins, put people at a psychological disadvantage. The chair also rocked whichever way you sat on it.

"What can I do for you, Mr. Pilkington?"

"It's about my wife. Is there any news at all?"

Collins shook his head, "She is still on the missing Persons list. Seemingly left of her own accord. Not really a police matter. More a domestic dispute… We are only interested if an offence against law has been committed."

Henry nodded sadly, "I know that is how it looks… but I *do* know my wife. She was a difficult person to live with, but there was love there. She wouldn't have left me, and her home. She thought a lot of her home, and she certainly wouldn't have disappeared without contacting her mother. Her trips to see her mother were the only cause of any friction we experienced. I have waited a long time now, and, I am sure some harm must have come to her. Is there no trace of her car?"

Collins shook his head," If we hear anything we'll let you know at once."

Collins stood up, but, Henry persisted he had a few more seeds to sow.

"How long does a person have to be missing before you people believe some harm may have come to them?" He remained seated and injected anger into his voice. "Surely people don't just disappear into thin air and the Police just shrug their shoulders?"

"Look Mr. Pilkington," Collins struggled to contain his patience, "Your wife left home in a normal way. Allegedly to visit her mother. We have spoken to the people next door, Mr. and Mrs... I forget their names."

"Moore," offered, Henry helpfully.

Collins nodded, "That's it, Moore, and they overheard a conversation which confirms that. More of her clothes were taken, more than she usually takes, you, yourself pointed that out. She is a mature person with no history of mental problems, so we can assume she knew exactly what she was doing, and the money she had in her account was drawn out the same day she disappeared. Every indication is that she *meant* to leave you. I'm sorry but..." Collins looked sympathetically at Henry's sorrowful face... "She could be anywhere... no hospital has reported an accident admission answering her description. I agree that not contacting her mother is strange... especially as they were so close, but then her mother is not exactly a rational thinking person is she?" Collins thumbed over the file. "As I recall she alleged all sorts of horrible things about you. Obviously the reaction of a very spiteful person. Nothing she said was substantiated, obviously whether you would agree with that assessment of her mother I don't know. Perhaps your wife was fed up with her mother, spiteful people are, let's say, unreliable contacts." Collins broke off lamely.

Henry nodded reluctantly, "She is a very difficult person, we have never hit it off but, Hannah was different, they seemed to understand each other. I am sure she has been killed, murdered or something. There is no other explanation."

Collins stood up, again, "I'm afraid, until we find some new evidence we cannot act on that theory... if we assumed that every missing person had been done to death we would need a Police force ten times the size, and at least ten days every week. I promise you we will not lose sight of this case and as soon as anything crops up, anything at all, we will let you know immediately." Collins sat down and busied himself with a sheaf of papers. Henry left.

Mentally rubbing his hands, the first step had been successful, Henry caught the bus into Coventry and made his way to the car park where he had left Hannah's car. It was still there, smothered with dust and the tyres were soft. He hoped the battery wasn't flat. He unlocked the car climbed in and switched on. The car fired and then stopped. He tried again... and again. Suddenly with a sputter the small engine started. He coaxed it for a minute or so. At the exit he was delayed for twenty minutes while a check was made for his allegedly lost ticket. It cost, Henry £12.00 Well worth it, he reasoned. At a garage he topped up the water and inflated the tyres, drove through the car wash and drove off, well pleased. At the railway station, he parked in the forecourt, another impersonal place, free of charge this time, and caught the train to Leamington Spa. From there he sported a taxi and arrived home enthused with the first stage of his new intrigue.

It was nightfall before he returned to Leamington. In a paper wrapping, he carried the original number plates of Hannah's car, and a small screwdriver. He drove back to the outskirts of Hampton Pogmore pulled into a dark farm track and changed the plates back to the originals. Then he unwrapped another article. Before leaving for Coventry he had again visited Fred Perkins shed in the graveyard. When borrowing the wheelbarrow he had noticed and old jacket and a worn cap which Fred wore in the colder weather. Henry stuffed it n his pocket, it looked like Fred, just the thing anyone in the village would recognize it. He stuffed it in between the seats. He remembered a small track which, during the Summer, children played, but no more. mother were too frightened to leave their children unattended. The track fell away into a shallow valley thickly covered with undergrowth. Blackberries were plentiful but too inaccessible for them to be picked. As it was on route to Hannah's mother it was the ideal place. With a final check Henry shoved the car forward into the valley. The Fiesta rolled hesitantly forward to the sloping bank, gathered speed, and ploughed into the undergrowth, slowly tipping on to its side and was almost enveloped by blackberry brambles and clinging foliage. Henry rubbed his hands... perfect.

Back home, Henry reviewed the situation. They would find the car before long. Someone always did. Then the Police would contact him. He had his story ready. No accusations, just hints. A search of the area would reveal no body, a search of the car would reveal the cap. Henry would grudgingly admit it looked like, Fred Perkins cap. Just a suggestion. Fred would panic, tell all, and show where, Hannah's body was and accuse Henry. He chuckled.

"Who the Hell would believe that story", he said to himself. Who better than a gravedigger to pop a body into a grave. Especially one who had recently approached the Bank for a loan. He thanked his lucky stars he had done nothing about the loan. That would have looked fishy. Now he could refuse Perkins politely and firmly. Let the little bastard get out of that! The £550 he had retrieved from Hannah's account on the day she disappeared, by fiddling her cheque through the system would be motive enough. £550 to Fred Perkins was a fortune, enough to whet his appetite for more. Henry went to bed and slept a dreamless sleep for the first time in weeks.

Chapter 11

Lost and Found

The Police did find the car. Or at least had it reported to them by a courting couple. Considering the place was remote enough to justify their sexual gyrations during daylight hours, they had enjoyed an hour of the summer sunshine not ten feet from where the Fiesta had slid over the bank. Had the young lady not lost a shoe over the edge, the car may well have lain there undetected. As it was they decided to tell Police, the undergrowth was too thick for them to see if there was anyone in the car. There were not too many reasons for them to be in the spot together. Not that would be believed. Sergeant Collins telephoned Henry at the Bank.

"There is no sign of your wife Sir. Perhaps you could call in at the Station just to make sure it is your wife's car. The registration checks out but we would like to be sure."

The dented Fiesta stood forlornly in the Station car park. Henry sadly confirmed it was. He peered inside unhappily, appearing to look for any of Hannah's belongings. He stepped out holding the cap.

"Yes Sergeant, this is Hannah's car, but there is nothing of hers inside. She carried a little mascot, a small dog that's not there. No handbag, nothing, only this thing which is certainly not hers." He passed the cap to Collins. "She must have had an accident. Where did you find the car?"

Collins told him. "It's been checked for prints, nothing to tell us anything."

Henry frowned, "I don't know exactly where you mean? Off the road you say? She must have lost control. Hannah was not a very good driver."

"About a hundred yards off the main road over a steep incline smothered in undergrowth. Not an accident. More a case of it having been pushed there. We have had ten men searching the area, just in case, but I shouldn't think your wife is there. The windows are intact, the doors closed but not locked. She couldn't have been thrown out."

"What are you saying Sergeant, that she was abducted and the car hidden?"

"Looks that way. Hardly think your wife would have shoved her car over the edge. This is not yours Sir?" He held out the cap.

Henry laughed mirthlessly, "Certainly not, never seen that before. Looks like a labourers cap, sort of thing old Fred Perkins would wear, the local gravedigger. Funnily it looks like him." Henry smiled. "Silly isn't it how you associate ideas. Fred Perkins, huh?"

Collins looked serious. This does put a different complex on things Mr. Pilkington, rather indicates that there could be foul play. We shall, of course treat your wife's disappearance as a more serious matter. You're sure you've never seen this cap before?"

Henry shook his head. "I certainly haven't, and Hannah would never allow such a thing in her car. Far too fussy."

Henry hurried home and imparted the news to Mary Moore, not only because he wanted her to know but because he wanted the whole village to know as soon as possible. Mary was the fastest means of communication known to man, including television. That afternoon by appointment, Fred Perkins called at the Bank and ushered into Henry's office. Henry took the bull by the horns.

"I'm sorry Mr. Perkins the Bank does not feel it can consider your application for a loan. Your credit rating and financial circumstances do not permit us to advance you that sum of money."

Fred Perkins looked aghast.

"What d'yer think y'er playing at Pilkington? Don't y'er come that with me! You do what I say, or it will be the bloody worse for you. Either you comes across with the money, or I'm off down the Police Station saarf-anoon, don't you play any games with me."

"You must do as you wish Mr. Perkins... I do not intend to be threatened by you. Good afternoon." Henry rose and opened the door. Perkins, his face black with anger, walked out, turning in the doorway.

"Right, you've bloody asked for it Pilkington, down the pipes you go, and good riddance." He stamped out of the Bank.

"Not one of your happiest customers Mr. Pilkington?" grinned Cynthia, Henry's secretary, watching the retreating Perkins.

"He's the local gravedigger, wanted a personal

loan, for £5,000. Most upset when I said no."

Sergeant Collins, accompanied by Detective Constable Wilbur Jones called on Henry three days later. Henry had been expecting something of the sort and was quite relaxed and prepared. He ushered the Police Officers into the lounge. Collins looked very concerned.

"I won't beat about the bush, Sir." He sat himself in an easy chair. Some very strange allegations have been made that I would like to discuss with you. Your hunch about that cap you found in your wife's car... a hunch that it looked like Fred Perkins, the gravedigger!"

Henry nodded. "Just a silly passing thought really."

"Perhaps not quite so silly. Mr. Perkins came to the station two days ago, I interviewed him, seems a bit of a nutter. Alleged you had strangled your wife and hidden her body in someone else's grave in the Churchyard? Says he found the body when the bulldozer ran amok and slammed into the church. Then he said he put the body back in the grave for Chris-sake! Says you know all about it and offered him money to keep his mouth shut. Says he refused and came to the Police instead?"

"Very law abiding of him I'm sure," Henry laughed out loud. He was surprised how natural the laugh sounded. "You have got to be joking Sergeant, what is this some sort of April fool stunt?"

Collins looked uncomfortable, "I'm afraid not. I only wish it was. The thing is that the cap does belong to him, he admitted it, and said it was pinched from his tool shed. He doesn't know when. We had it examined, found traces of earth on the peak, all over it in fact. Clay soil, same as the graveyard. Anyway he agrees it is his."

Henry shook his head in bewilderment, "I'm sorry Sergeant, I don't understand all this. Why on earth would someone like, Fred Perkins make such a shocking allegation? He has always seemed such a pleasant little man. I've certainly had very little to do with him except..."

"Except what Sir?" Collins fastened on Henry's hesitation.

"Banking business really Sergeant... not relative at all, comes under the heading of confidential."

"Nothing confidential in the light of these allegations, what were you going to say?"

"Well Mr. Perkins did apply for a loan recently, he needed money apparently, I had to refuse him. He did not qualify. He was rather put out I'm afraid, and abusive."

"I see..." Collins looked thoughtful. "Unfortunately we shall have to apply for an exhumation order to check out these malicious allegations. There is a lot we need to check out!"

"Exhumation order. Surely you don't believe my wife really is in the graveyard?" Henry looked distressed.

"We must check, Mr. Pilkington... the order is necessary because we need to open an authentic grave. Consecrated ground and all that. I'm sure we shall find nothing, but we must check."

Henry shrugged. "Do you think this Perkins fellow knows anything about my wife's disappearance?"

Hard to tell, very strange that his cap should be in her car. Strange that he should be in need of money when your wife was in possession of a rather large amount, apparently. Strange that he should make these outrageous allegations. Leave it with us Sir."

The Police left and Henry helped himself to a drink. Everything was going to plan. Hannah *was* discovered just as, Perkins had said. Her remains were taken to the Hospital mortuary where, Henry was asked to identify her. He broke down in grief and was taken home by Police car and Mary was summoned to care for him. He stayed indoors for a week, and received the total sympathy of the Bank staff, and most of the villagers who attended the funeral, following the autopsy. Hannah was laid to rest a few feet from Maud Hodge.

Police broke the news to, Hannah's mother, who collapsed in a hysterical fit. There was no consoling her, especially when she was told that she could not view the body. (Hannah's remains were badly affected by being shuttled around the graveyard and exposed to the air.) In view of her mother state of mind the Doctor advised against it, fearing a heart attack, and administered a sedative. She was, however, allowed to attend the funeral. She was brought to the graveside by a Police woman and apart from sobbing she glared with venom at Henry who kept well away. Fearing she may suddenly fly at Henry she was swiftly taken to the Police car and taken home.

'Let's hope this is the last bloody time thought, Henry hanging his head in grief, he felt a twinge of conscience seeing his mother in law in such a state. Fred Perkins was arrested and charged with murder in the first degree and remanded in custody. He was to be sentenced in three weeks time. Henry relaxed.

Chapter 12

Loose Ends

"Oh Come on Sarge, it's an open and shut case. Stone bonker... slam dunk. He'll go down. Got to, we've got all the evidence we need. Almost a confession, leaving his cap at the scene of the crime!"

Collins glared at D.C. Wilbur Jones... "You'll never make Sergeant as long as you accept the obvious. There's something bloody fishy about all this. Too good to be true." He slammed the door in frustration.

"Answer me this Mr. Clever arse. One, how did the car get to the ditch. Perkins can't drive... never has driven, we know that, he would have piled the car up before he got there."

"An accomplice?" Wilbur offered.

"Perhaps." Collins admitted, "If he knocked her

off how did he get to the graveyard without being seen. You can't go hiking around with a dead'un over your shoulder... not round here you can't, they can see a runny nose at fifty paces."

"Perhaps he knocked her off in the graveyard before he drove off in the car... or his mate did?"

"What the Hell was she doing in the graveyard in the first place? Off to see her mother she was, not doing her brass rubbings. Two, why leave your cap in the car if you're not driving it yourself? This bloody cap bugs me! Pilkington identified it straight away very fucking coincidental, that."

"Could she have pulled it off in the struggle?"

Collins snorted. "Pilkington did this! Sure as my arse faces South. Get your coat we're going to do some legwork. This has been carefully planned. Perkins hasn't got enough brain cells to work this out."

Before they left the station, Collins inspected the Fiesta for the fourth time.

"Look at it, clean as a new pin, been in the bushes for six weeks and still shines like a whores eyes. Topped up with petrol, oil and water and the tyres up to pressure. The only place that's grotty are the number plates, muck down the sides of the raised letters, but not, and I repeat not, in the screw slots... they've been off recently."

His colleague looked puzzled but said nothing.

"Let's go and see the Vicar." said Collins.

The Vicar was standing in the sunshine admiring the underpinning of the Church. He was well pleased with the claim against the Council. They had assured him that all would be put to rights. Fortunately it was not possible to repair just the damage the Bulldozer had done, before that could take place, some internal rotting had to be fixed. All was grist to the mill of the Reverend Smallfoot. He was happy to speak with the two Police Officers and expound upon the disaster in great detail.

"I dare say you had a load of gawping sightseers Vicar?"

"Only at first, the villagers are very good, kept away when we asked. It was very dangerous you know... anyone injured would have been a catastrophe. As it was the Lord protected us all. Only Mr. Pilkington who came to express his regrets, so kind he made a donation."

Mr. Pilkington, one of your regulars? Has a lot to do with the Church?" Collins ears had pricked up.

The Reverend smiled," No I rarely see him. Busy man I suppose. Not one of my flock so to speak, but it shows how the distress of others prompts the flow of human kindness."

Collins sniffed, "Did Mr. Pilkington have any special reason to visit the scene so quickly? A loved one buried perhaps, some personal interest?"

"No I don't think so. I feel it was a gesture from a respected member of the village. One never knows who one's friends are Sergeant. We live in a cloud of indifference I'm afraid, unwilling to make the first move. Christ was never like that he approached all men on equal terms."

"Where did Mr. Pilkington look first?" interjected Collins quickly... If he wasn't careful he'd finish up getting both barrels of a mothering Sunday Sermon.

"I think he was just generally interested," the Vicar was puzzled, "I confess he did venture towards poor Maud Hodges resting place, I had to caution him of the danger. Poor Maud was, how would you say, in the firing line of the bulldozer, her grave bore the full brunt. The grave the Council were kind enough to repair under the Tent last week." The Vicar had no idea of the reason for the exhumation, he would have had an attack of the vapours otherwise. "It was of no consequence Sergeant," he smiled, "The earthly resting place is merely a hesitation in the journey to everlasting joy."

"Quite so," muttered, Collins, "Rather like a bus shelter while you wait for a number 9 bus."

"How quaint," beamed the Vicar.

"Thanks for your help Vicar." Collins shook hands and led Jones towards the car.

"Any longer and we would have been signed up for the choir." The D.C. grinned.

"Don't be sacrilegious you bloody little atheist." retorted Collins.

Later Sergeant Collins glared at the unfortunate, Fred Perkins in the interview room of the County prison.

"Knackered you are Fred... well and truly knackered. How old are you, 46 you'll be over 60 when you next see the light of day. No more graves to dig then. Everyone will have been off to the moon."

"I never done it Sir," muttered Fred. He looked haggard and miserable in his prison clothes, his lips had drooped into a perpetual sulk and he looked near to tears.

"Course you fuckin did!" Collins turned his back and sauntered across to the barred window.

"I never did." Fred summoned enough energy to shout, "It was that bloody, Pilkington! He did it. Just like I said... he wrung er neck, no one believes me! Es an important man ee is. I ain't nuffin, that's me. But im, they believes im fuckin bastard!"

"How much do you earn Fred?" Collins turned to face the unhappy man. "How much do you take home in readies… hard cash?"

"Forty pounds," muttered Fred.

"How much rent do you pay?"

"Nuffin' I gets the house rent free from the Church."

"What else do you get from the Church?"

"Nuffin. Just a meal now and then, and what the Vicar gives me, which ain't much."

Collins looked at him quietly. "What would you do with £5,000 Fred?"

Fred looked uncomfortable… "Go on oliday… buy some decent grub… new boots an dat." His voice tailed off.

"Where on holiday?"

"Oh. I don't really know. Weston I suppose. Weston on the Mare."

"Weston Super mare?" Assisted Collins gently.

Fred you wouldn't recognize £5,000 if it reared up and bit you. Even a fiver is a lot of money to you... What made you ask for all that money?"

"I've told you I need a oliday. Never ad an oliday. Never ad nuffin, nor as my missus.... worked ard and saved a bit, but still ad nuffin. I thought I would ask for a loan. It's in the papers... They offer loans. The banks offer loans, I just thought..."

"£5,000 Fred? 5,000 coins all piled up, they'd fill your loo and the garden shed as well. Come on, you thought that was the sort of money Pilkington would understand, that's why you picked that amount. You were blackmailing him weren't you?"

"No Sir I was not."

"Fred!!!"

"Not blackmail, not blackmail." Fred collapsed.

"I thought he would pay me money to keep quiet, that's all."

"That is blackmail Fred. Pure and simple." Collins felt sorry for the dispirited and woebegone man.

Wilbur Jones who had been standing in the corner, "I think he's telling the truth sarge." He murmured.

Collins glared at him, "If it's any consolation I think so too," looking Fred in the eye. "I believe, Pilkington murdered his wife, and I intend to prove it, but it isn't easy, not after what you've done, Perkins. One thing puzzles me. How was it that you suspected Pilkington in the first place?"

"It was his habit. He was like a robot, left home at the same time in his car, came home at exactly the same time, never different. I saw him walking home, I'd been up the Goose for a pint, late at night, no car. Same time I..."

Fred's eyes lit up with hope. "I'll do anything Mr. Collins, I don't want to go to prison. What about my missus and everything?"

"Bit late hunny, bit too late. You can't go around blackmailing people, no matter what they've done... and popping stiffs back underground just because they look untidy. Now then why don't you tell us everything that happened and I'll see what I can do. Few years ago and they would have topped you. Put a bag over your head and dropped you through a hole in the scaffold, been too late to do anything then."

Collins waited quietly whilst Fred composed himself, he then blurted out the whole story. How he had found Hannah in the bulldozer scoop and decided to blackmail Henry. Collins listened without comment. Nodding his head as Fred's story corroborated his own feelings and assumptions.

Chapter 13

Open House

"You were right then sarge. Reckon it was Pilkington." The D.C. looked at Collins with admiration as they drove away from the prison.

"Course I'm bloody right! That's why I'm a Sergeant and you're not. Too bloody convenient, facts in a murder are never that easy, because everyone lies. Even the innocent because no-one is ever completely innocent. Always got something to hide, even if it's only having it off with the baby-sitter."

"What's next sarge?" The D.C. was keen to get on with things now there was a bit more meat in the situation.

Collins looked thoughtful," I don't know, we haven't got any real evidence. Whether we believe Pilkington did it or not, doesn't alter the facts. If we took Pilkington in front of the Magistrates at this point there would be Hell to pay. The case would be chucked out and we'd be done for false arrest. The bastard's safe, the only thing that can implicate him is the evidence of Perkins who is an almost convicted murderer. Fat lot of good that is!"

"But it stands out a mile sarge, obvious, now we've looked into it all."

"Circumstantial my friend, just circumstantial evidence that's all. How did Perkins know it was Pilkington, he didn't see him." He frowned in concentration.

"What if we..." Offered the D.C.

"Shut up while I think... can't think with you rabbiting on all the time." Wilbur shut up.

Sergeant Collins suddenly swung the car round towards Warwick. He hadn't spoken for ten minutes and then a sudden decision resulted in a totally illegal U turn and they headed towards Warwick Hospital.

"We're off to see the Pathologist, providing he's not pissed or watching Coronation Street." With that the D.C. had to be content. He ventured one comment.

"We've seen the pathology report."

"All that said was that she was dead and had been strangled with a chunk of rope. A chimpanzee could have decided that."

The Pathology Department was almost in darkness when they arrived but, luckily Doctor Douglas Macintosh, was still in his office. He looked up crossly as they knocked on his door.

"Come in," he called in a broad Scottish accent, heavy with impatience.

"Ah. Sergeant Collins... to what do I owe the displeasure of seeing you?"

"Some help Doctor, a few more facts about the Pilkington murder."

"You had all the facts before you charged, Perkins... if that was his name."

"New evidence, some corroboration of possible circumstances."

The Doctor sniffed, "Changed ye mind have yer?"

"Something like that." Nodded Collins, "We only have details of the cause of death, we didn't really need more than that at the time. Perhaps you did a more detailed examination of clothing and other marks?"

Collins looked hopeful. Macintosh glared at him from below bushy eyebrows, his lips set in a firm and belligerent line. "Young man if I carry out an autopsy on anyone, I examine everything. I am not interested in proving anything for the benefit of your ability to charge someone or exonerate them. My job is to uncover even the most minute fragment of knowledge about the cadaver. As a result I get to know more about them than they knew themselves, or that any other Doctor could determine whilst they were still alive. If you are too carried away with the need to add another feather to your cap and fail to absorb the facts that I present, or even bother to read them, that must be your problem."

Collins endeavoured to placate the Doctor, without success as he rose, and withdrew a thick file from the filing cabinet in the corner of his office.

"I imagine," Macintosh said with heavy sarcasm, "that if I leave you to read the whole thing you will, again, pick out the pieces you need without reading them in context, therefore in the interests of medicine I will explain the implications of certain findings. You had better sit down."

They sat down. Doctor Macintosh adjusted a pair of half-moon spectacles half way down his nose and opened the file.

"I will dispense with the facts that you have obviously taken enough interest to note. Mrs. Pilkington was strangled with a piece of soft rope, or thick string would around her neck from behind. The rope used was soft, this is indicated by the width of the abrasions and the torn skin. Anything hard would have bitten more deeply and involved a higher degree of deep tissue damage."

"You say from behind?" ventured Collins.

Macintosh nodded, "Sometimes victims are strangled from the front. Invariably this takes the form of manual strangulation, thumbs pressed into the throat, the action of an assailant suddenly losing control. To strangle from behind indicates a premeditated intent. Enough to say she was asphyxiated... choked to death. There were bruises to the buttocks, the skin was burned across both heels and on one elbow."

"Burned?" Questioned, Collins incredulously.

"Superficial friction burns, I will come to that in a moment, and her ear, right ear, was lacerated. She was wearing a cashmere cardigan and a woollen skirt, her tights were torn and her finger nails disclosed minute particles of a powder. This powder turned out to be carpet cleaner. The sort of things ladies puff across the carpet and then extract it again with a vacuum cleaner."

Collins opened his mouth to ask a question but closed it again as the Doctor fastened with a glare.

"From these findings," Macintosh went on, "it is reasonable to assume that the woman was attacked from behind and dragged across the floor, bruising her buttocks in her struggle for life, and skinning her heels as she was dragged across the carpet. The carpet was of a high nylon content which burned as she was dragged. The woman fought hard and the assailant was in a hysterical panic. The act of a frightened man. I say man because there are few women who could have exerted the strength necessary to drag a terrified nine stone body across the floor which is what happened. Her skirt and cardigan disclosed more traces of the powder and fibres from a reasonably little worn carpet. These are available if you so wish." The Doctor closed the file.

"I believe she was wrapped in a blanket Doctor. Did you examine that?" Collins could have bitten his tongue out.

"Do you never listen man?" Macintosh roared, "only five minutes ago I clearly told you that I examine everything!"

Collins grinned sheepishly.

"The blanket came from a bed I imagine. Probably an under blanket because there were dead mites in the fibres."

"Dead mites?" The Detective constable spoke for the first time.

"Every night we all shed skin in minute fragments." Doctor Macintosh removed his spectacles and polished them on his tie. "This skin produces mites which live off the dead scaling. They get in the mattresses, duvets, pillows and sheets, and they thrive in the warmth and humidity. If the average housewife realized she was sleeping in a mass of writhing life she would have hysterics." For the first time he chuckled at the look of shock on the D.C.'s face. "It is not as bad as you imagine. They are so small many thousands could run about on a pin head and frequent vacuuming gets rid of a few million every time. But, they are there, and, an irrefutable indication that the blanket came from a bed." The Doctor sat back and gazed at the two policemen. "I can go on with details of the condition of the deceased's internal organs, the quality of her toe nails, and the contents of her stomach, her lungs were wholesome, unlike yours Sergeant. The nicotine stains on your fingers, indicate that you have little regard for your life."

Collins wriggled uncomfortably. "Thank you very much for your time Doctor, and your patience." He rose to leave.

"Come again when you change your mind again." The sarcasm rang in their ears.

"Bloody wars I wouldn't like to really upset the old codger." Jones said as they left the Hospital. "Tear you up for arse paper, he would."

"Teach you to read everything in the post mortem report won't it." Retorted Collins.

"You had it first," complained Jones. "I thought

you had done that?"

"Never leave to others, my son."

Detective Chief Inspector Vale closed the report and looked at Sergeant Collins.

"I think you're right... your assessment of what really happened, and that, Pilkington did it is correct. The evidence of the post mortem more or less clinches it, that the murder took place indoors, but it is all circumstantial.

Circumstantial evidence, allegations and hunches are not enough Sergeant, they won't hold up in Court. A good lawyer will tear you to pieces, and we'll all look fools. Besides it will only strengthen the case against Perkins. Bring me some proof and all this will slot neatly into place, a confession volunteered without duress, as all you can do is ask for a further remand in custody for Perkins when he comes up tomorrow."

"But it would, at least, show that, Perkins

didn't do it, won't it?"

"Doesn't prove anything, one way or another, just a lot of wishful thinking. Think of a way to seriously disturb Pilkington?"

"Put the shits up him... I really mean up him. That's what must be done."

Sergeant spoke more to himself than to his colleague. They were seated in the window seat of the, "Goose and Duckling," contemplating the diminishing levels in their pints of best bitter.

"We need the carpet, or some of it."

"What carpet?" The D.C. asked, frowning in puzzlement.

"The, Pilkington carpet... the one he dragged her backside across." The constable still looked puzzled. "So that Scottish butcher can examine it... Confirm that it is the same carpet that left dust, and threads, in old, Ma Pilkington's skirt stupid."

"Can't we get a search warrant?"

Collins shook his head. "Chief wants more evidence first. Even if we prove the carpet matches the threads in the skirt, they'll say it could have happened before, could have slipped on er arse the week before or something."

"What about the blanket she was wrapped in?" The D.C wriggled his shoulders uncomfortably, he still had visions of millions of bed mites writhing about in his own bed. "We could prove that it was his."

Collins wrinkled his nose. "Too weak... too many loopholes for some smart arse lawyer to pull to bits. No it has to be a confession, willingly and freely made."

"Some bloody opes... who's going to confess to that lot? Volunteer for 15 years in the pokey, ave to be round the bend or frightened out of his life."

Sergeant looked at, Jones strangely. His eyes

were intense.

Jones shifted uncomfortably... "I only said..."

"I know what you said." Murmured, Collins quietly. "Detective Constable, Jones you may well have made the brightest observation you have ever made in your miserable career, but, there may be hope for you yet."

Collins stood up. "I shall buy the beer." he remarked magnanimously and carried the glasses to the bar. The D.C. stared unbelievingly.

Charter 14

Proof

Mrs. Bunting, (Hannah's mother) answered the door irritably wiping her hands on a tea towel. She was far from pleased to see Sergeant Collins and the D.C.

"Oh! It's you again... I thought that awful little beast should have been hanged by now? I really can't get myself all upset again, I' m not well, and all this has been too much for me. What do you want this time?"

"Just a cup of your superb coffee Mrs. Bunting."

The Sergeant beamed his finest hypocritical smile at the cross woman and watched her relax a little. "We are on your side you know... wouldn't dream of causing you any more suffering. Goodness knows you've had enough to put up with. I admire you, the way you have stood up to everything, not many women would have done it. I admire you, I really do."

Mrs. Bunting looked at him suspiciously, but there was no sign of a smirk, he looked very sincere. She sniffed and smoothed her skirt. "Well you'd better come in then."

As she busied herself making coffee Constable, Jones looked at, Collins with admiration. "I have never heard such a load of bloody bullshit in my life. Makes all the politicians green with envy." He grinned.

Collins bared his teeth. When coffee was being sipped with excessive appreciation by the Sergeant he looked at Mrs. Bunting with sincerity.

"We need your help Mrs. Bunting. Without you we can't bring the beast who murdered your daughter to justice. He will go scot-free, even worse an innocent party will pay for a crime he didn't commit."

Hannah s' mother put down her cup very slowly. "Whatever are you saying, you have arrested that man, Perkins, or whatever his name is, the one who digs the graves." She shuddered."He killed my, Hannah, or so you said?"

Collins shook his head, "No he didn't. It was, Henry Pilkington, your son in law. He killed, Hannah. We know it, we are certain, but, we can't prove it."

Mrs. Bunting sank back in her chair, her face went ashen, her mouth dropped open and tears filled her eyes. "Oh God,! Oh my God!... Oh my dear girl. Her own husband!"

Collins was on his feet and took her hand. "I'm so sorry to give you that news, we are very sure." He grinned to himself as he saw the glint appear in her tearful eyes and he felt the anger stiffen her pudgy fingers. He'd summed the old girl up very accurately. He sat down again.

"The swine. The filthy swine. I knew it. I had that feeling all along, but no-one would listen." She composed herself and was visibly transposing shock and grief into hatred of, Henry. "I could tell when he telephoned and said Hannah was to come home. There was something in his voice, he knew she wasn't here. Hadn't been here, all the time she was lying there horribly mutilated." She covered her face and choked, but not for long, she wanted to hear more. "Have you arrested him? Is he in prison? The beast should be murdered himself."

Collins drew his chair nearer to her, "You can help us put him in prison, if you will, I'll explain what I mean."

She nodded vigorously. "Anything… I'll do anything for my Hannah." She dried her eyes and sniffed.

Collins began to talk, he told her everything they suspected, outlined exactly how the murder had been committed and covered all the reasons why, Perkins had been arrested. She sat transfixed, emitting sobs and sighs at the right moments and soaking up all the information into her seething mind.

"This is what I want you to do, Mrs. Bunting," ended Collins, swallowing the last of his, now cold coffee, "If you would like to help..."

She couldn't have been more willing if there had been £10,000 at the end of it.

Malicious old bag, thought Jones, if Hannah had been formed in her mother's likeness then, Henry's action should be justifiable homicide.

Chapter 15

Pressured

Two days later, Henry received another devastating shock to his already overloaded cardiac system. As he opened the door to leave for the Bank he was stupefied by the sight of Hannah's mother striding purposefully along the path to the front door, carrying a suitcase. Although the continued remand in custody for Fred Perkins mystified him somewhat, by now the little sod should have been charged, Henry had managed to convince himself that there was nothing to worry about. Certain twinges of conscience took place over the ultimate fate of the miserable little gravedigger, but he bolstered his feelings with resentment of the attempt at blackmail. Even more his need for personal preservation helped to quell his guilt. The sight of, Hannah's mother was the last straw. Damn the bloody woman... what the Hell did she want. Scenes at the funeral had been bad enough. They had parted on strained terms, neither wishing to set eyes on the other again. Now the cow had appeared again! Henry couldn't believe it. Her first words shook him even more...

"I'm here... and I've come to stay, Henry Pilkington, whether you like it or not. You took my daughter away from me, left me to fend for myself, so you can damned well look after me."

She tossed her head in defiance and swept around, Henry and into the open front door before he could utter a word. Henry dragged his senses back and slammed into the house after her, thudding the door closed behind him. He was furious, but cautious, the words, you took my daughter away, screamed at him. What the Hell did she mean?

"How dare you Agnes", he snarled at her. "How dare you come into my home like this, demanding this and demanding that. You have no right here! Hannah is here no longer. I want nothing more to do with you, any settlement of, Hannah's property will be dealt with in the proper way, you needn't think you're getting anything else."

Agnes Bunting threw her raincoat on to the back of the chair and swung towards him. She placed her hands on her ample hips and looked at him with scorn. He was disturbed by the venom and hatred in her eyes. He felt mentally naked under her scrutiny.

"Now you listen to me, you murderer," she hissed, "I know what happened to my Hannah. I know you murdered her, not that poor little man in prison. You. You were the one who killed her. She can't pay you back, but I can, and, in her memory I am going to do so."

She stalked off into the kitchen and put the kettle on. The days that followed were unbearable to Henry. Agnes Bunting enveloped the house. She was everywhere, fastidious and precise to an extreme that, Hannah would have envied. The morning mail and the newspaper were collected almost before they hit the mat and secreted somewhere until the evening when he returned from work. No matter how, Henry complained and berated her, it made no difference. His meal was ready as he walked in the door and he ate alone, Agnes had eaten and cleared up before his return. There was no television, not that, Henry could have concentrated, and as soon as he finished eating the plate was swept away. Any whisky which he attempted to hide in order to soften his miserable existence was confiscated and no pleasures were allowed. Henry had no option but to suffer. He was terrified of her knowledge of his activities and the possibility that she would go to the Police and expose him. Each day he would be subjected to a report of the latest conversation which had taken place between, Agnes and her departed daughter.

"Hannah asked me today to avoid using that easy chair, the one you strangled her from. And you must buy another under-blanket for the spare bed. Hannah told me you used the old one to wrap her in." Henry rushed upstairs and was violently sick. The fucking woman was psychic!

"Hannah wants to know if the money you took from her account would be included in her estate? It was her money after all."

Agnes warmed to her task and was able, possibly because she had known her daughter so well, to slot in items about which she had no accurate knowledge, and hit the nail on the head. "You didn't water the primula as she asked!"

Henry was going mad. He knew it, felt it, his brain was either a numb blob, or an electric storm. He began to believe that, Agnes was actually talking to, Hannah. He heard, Agnes talking in the night, she would chuckle and chat into the early hours. Her voice penetrated the thin walls so he heard her parting comment.

"Take care up there my dear it must be very strange for you."

He was viewed with concern by those at the Bank. His superiors cast suspicious eyes on his work and the secretaries voiced the opinion that, Pilky was not only over the hill, but sliding rapidly down the other side.

"Must be the male menopause," grinned Jenny.

"Only male who ever paused with me," giggled Jane.

Henry collapsed from inside. His stamina faded completely. He couldn't sleep, and was placed sick by the Bank. In the early hours of Thursday he walked, and walked and became disorientated. He found himself at the doors of the Police Station, a haggard and thin replica of himself. He asked to see Detective Collins. The Sergeant on duty looked at Henry with concern. Christ, what a wreck he looked, never seen anyone like that outside the morgue.

"Sergeant Collins won't be in before 9am Sir. Can I help?"

The Sergeant really wanted to help. Henry shook his head, "I'll wait. I can't go home. I'll wait, can I wait?" He looked pleadingly at the sympathetic face.

"Course you can, no drunks tonight they don't get paid until later. Make yourself comfortable in the cell. I'll make you a cuppa, you look done in."

Henry nodded and followed the officer to the cells behind the office. He collapsed on the bunk and failed to hear the arrival of the steaming cup of tea. At 7am he woke up. The cell door had been pushed shut and Henry saw the bars. Huge unbending bars bearing down on him, encircling him, restricting him, shutting him away from life and air, from his very existence. Adrenalin pulsed into his brain and limbs, restoring a clear thinking process for the first time in weeks. Nothing, nothing was worth a life like this. He burst open the door and sprawled into the passage way clawing his way out, had to get out, out into whatever awaited him, nothing could be worse than the slamming assault of those bars. He rushed into the street, his mind screaming in panic. He had almost begged to stay in a place like that. He stopped and took some very deep breaths. A cold deliberation overtook him, Hannah blast her soul, had driven him to murder. Her mother was doing the same thing, the pair of them across the Great Divide, were in collusion, pushing him into madness. How did she know? How in Hell did she know? It didn't matter she did know, but she couldn't prove it. If she knew, then the Police knew. If they knew why hadn't he been arrested, because they couldn't bloody well prove it. Henry laughed, a hysterical high pitched laugh. As he walked homeward he summoned up a new strength. Spawned by the experience in the cell his instinct for self preservation strengthened. Why should he allow his fear to turn him into a snivelling doormat. As he let himself into the house he resolved to let them do their damnedest.

"Where have you been all night?" Mrs Bunting stood, formidable and imposing in the hallway, hands on hips.

Henry looked at her for a long cold moment. "Mind your own fucking business you cow. Get your things and be out of this house in five minutes. I have never laid a hand on your precious daughter, whatever you may think, but, as I live and breathe if I see your ugly face ever again I'll lay hands on you. I'll break your scrawny neck."

The hatred that emanated from, Henry was enough for Agnes Bunting. Sergeant Collins had warned her not to take chances. 'If he turns nasty, don't argue, just get out.'

She didn't argue, she scurried around and collected her case and the few belongings she had brought with her and sidled past Henry who stood, unmoving, in the hallway. The temptation to make a last cutting remark was too much for her. She turned to face, Henry and opened her mouth to speak. Henry gripped her shoulders and spun her round pushing her towards the open front door. At the same time he planted a full blooded kick on her very ample backside which sent the hapless Mrs. Bunting sprawling, face downward, on the path, her clothing and case scattering in all directions. Henry slammed the door. He felt better. A lot better, should have done that a long time ago. He felt so much better that he was tempted to open the door and have another go. Instead he made his way to the downstairs loo and lifted the lid off the cistern. Inside was a half bottle of Bells Whisky, firmly sealed in a plastic bag. Another strike for Henry.

Chapter 16

Mysterious

"I do not feel that the circumstances justify a further remand in custody." The Magistrate peered over his spectacles at Sergeant Collins, who fidgeted uncomfortably in the witness box. "It really is not the responsibility of the Court to grant unlimited periods of time for the Police to provide sufficient evidence to justify committal for trial. Do you have this evidence Sergeant?"

"Not totally your worship. There is a further charge to be brought which is linked to the original."

The Magistrate looked at the Police officer quizzically. "I will grant one further week. If you are not ready to proceed at that time I shall dismiss the case."

D.C. Jones joined, Collins as they left the Court.

"What now sarge? We ought to drop the charge against Perkins. Poor little sod is rotting away for nothing."

"Bloody blackmailer, that's what he is, serve him bloody right! Don't start feeling sorry for the villains of this benighted world my son or you'll finish up as bad as they are."

"Do you think, Pilkington will confess?"

"Let's go see." Grinned Collins, "apparently he staggered into the nick in the early hours, absolutely knackered, wanted to see me, rushed out again about 7am, slept in the cells. He looked like something risen from the dead, so the Station Officer reckoned. Yes my son I think he's about to clear his conscience."

Jones looked worried, "Could be said he confessed under duress, a couple of weeks with that old biddy is enough to send anyone to the funny farm."

"Nothing to do with us, if anyone can't get on with their mother in law it's got nothing to do with the Pillars of Public Morality."

"Who?"

"Us you fool."

Much to their amazement it was a very different Henry Pilkington who answered the door. He certainly looked haggard and tired, but there was an alertness in his eyes which caused the Policemen to drop their complacency.

"I believe you called at the Station, asking for me, early hours I'm told?"

"Indeed I did Sergeant. Please come in." Henry led the way into the lounge. Jones pulled a face.

"I was seeking advice." Henry gestured towards the easy chairs. "Advice as to whether I was able to call upon Police assistance to evict my late wife mother. She has been living here for the past two or three weeks and making my life a

151

misery. I wished her to leave, she has now done so, there is no need for Police action."

"Nothing to do with the Police anyway," commented Collins dryly," not unless there was unnecessary force used."

Henry laughed, "I wasn't likely to throw her out bodily."

Collins eyes narrowed. Too bloody confident was Henry. A new attitude. No sign of cracking as they had hoped.

"How was she objectionable Mr. Pilkington?"

The Sergeant decided to bait him a little. "You couldn't expect her to be full of the joys of spring with her daughter lying dead."

"Oh she had some ridiculous idea that I was involved in my wife's' death. Stupid of course, but she was a doting mother and had never had much time for me as a husband. Only natural that she should turn her venom on me I suppose.

Alleged she had spiritual conversations with Hannah which implicated me in, Jerkins' violence. Incidentally when does he go for trial?"

"He's still on remand, still more enquiries to be made."

Collins watched, Henry closely. He could have sworn such a remark would have given him a jolt. Nothing, just the ghost of a smile.

"Hannah mother mentioned that she spoke to you both just before she arrived here."

This was shot in the dark, this time it was Collins who was jolted, his eyes flickered with dismay. He had impressed on the bloody woman to say nothing about their allegations, or the hopeful outcome of her visit. Why can't women keep their bloody mouths shut. Before he could recover his thought, Jones spoke.

"She seemed very rational when we saw her." He could have bitten his tongue out as soon as he said it. Collins could have torn it out by the roots.

This time there was no doubt about the smile on Henry's face.

"So, it was a matter of collusion between Mrs. Bunting and yourselves. She said nothing of your visit in actual fact, just that her fatuous comments were flavoured with outside influences. If I can show that there was any chicanery taking place between she, and yourselves, with a view to exerting pressure on myself because of some damned fool idea that I was implicated, then it bodes ill for your integrity or the code of conduct normally associated with the Police. I suggest you both leave now and busy yourselves with the conviction of the guilty man. I shall consult a solicitor over your behaviour."

Outside the house, Collins vented his spleen on the unfortunate Jones.

"Of all the bloody damned fool comments to

make. Couldn't you see he was fishing! He didn't know for sure we had seen the blasted woman, you dropped us right in the shit, now we have no chance! Any hopes of a confession are straight down the tubes. Christ I wish you were a Sergeant so I could have you broken down to D.C."

Henry felt better than he had since the first day he contemplated murdering Hannah. He had the whip hand, they knew he had done it but couldn't prove it, shot their bolt, any evidence they did have would be inadmissible. Collusion with a key witness, priming her as to what to say! Henry rubbed his hands and chuckled. Fred Perkins was released. The charge of Blackmail dropped, as much of the offence was linked with the murder, without proof of that there was little chance of a conviction. Perkins seethed with resentment, weeks he had been cooped up in gaol, all for nothing, all because he was a nothing, not a toff like Pilkington. The Vicar took him back as a gravedigger and general handyman, rather against his innermost feelings but he hadn't been convicted, in the eyes of the law he was innocent. Who was the Vicar to judge his fellow man, let him who was without sin. Besides grave diggers were hard to find. Once a week, Henry dutifully carried flowers to, Hannah's grave. An act which, Mary Moore viewed with sympathy and duly informed the community of the devotion, Henry had for the inconsiderate woman. Fred Perkins watched with hatred.

"Bloody Hypocrite," he mouthed.

The Council workers, specially recruited to achieve speedy and efficient results with the damaged Church were progressing at their own speed. The damage to the outer wall had revealed some quite serious deterioration to the original woodwork. The infamous Death Watch Beetle had wreaked havoc to some of the supporting timbers. Unfortunately, time was short, and the foreman had in mind that there was a great deal of disruption scheduled for the surrounding villages. He quietly suggested that, as the Church had stood for 400 years without problems, to cover the rot would restore it to at least the same condition as it was before and that the time spent on trying to underpin it, would be costly and was just, well, not on.

In consequence the Reverend Smallfoot was delighted to see the façade of his Church resume a reasonable appearance, and a sturdy one. Services were resumed in full flight ready for the Pagan celebration of Pentecost.

Henry, in the meantime, was really feeling his feet, convinced that the Police had nothing to go on and that retribution was a thing of the past. He bought drinks in the Goose and Duckling quite regularly and became a character, of the village. He still ate with the Moores, one had to be circumspect. Feeling that he had a lot to thank the Church for, perhaps not in a spiritual manner exactly, he even attended Sunday morning service. With fond memories of the previous £20 the Reverend would cast welcoming looks directly at, Henry during the sermon. It was, ironically enough, a combination of spiritual fervour and influence from the Heavens which proved to be, Henry's undoing.

Coincidentally the Reverend Smallfoots sermon centred on the walls of Jericho and he felt the subject quite topical. It was also, Lifeboat Day, and he chose, "For Those in Peril on the Sea," as the major hymn. Martha Bloom, the regular organist was pleased. She knew the hymn by heart and enjoyed belting it out to the accompaniment of the congregation, who, knowing the words, could be depended upon to do justice to the hymn. Henry listened half heartedly to the Vicar and then rose to his feet as an almighty blast on the organ heralded the final hymn. Martha Bloom went to town, the windows rattled, the pews vibrated and flaked of ancient plaster fluttered down from above. The resonant voices from the men, some of whom had visited the, Goose and Duckling prior to Church, added to the swell of sound which would have put a large Disco to shame. The final verse was launched into with gusto and when finished, Martha continued urging the organ to greater efforts. The congregation became bemused, there were ominous signs from the building, creaks and sudden shocks. As one they made their way outside imagining an earthquake was on way. The Reverend called to pacify the crowd, but became frightened himself. Even, Martha stopped playing and joined in the sudden exodus. Henry was amongst the last to reach the comparative safety of the open air. Thrusting and pushing he was still unable to breach the wall of bodies and, Henry found himself under the buttresses of the gallery. The walls moved Henry swore they actually moved. He gazed upward as a marble Angel, the plaster securing her to the wall powdery and old, gave way, dived with hands outstretched in prayer. She struck Henry full on the back of his neck as he tried to duck, out of the way. His neck broke with a savage snap and the luckless man lay spread-eagled beneath the remains of a truly avenging heavenly host. Sergeant Collins gazed silently at the lifeless body of Henry Pilkington as it lay, pallid and sightless in the mortuary.

"Makes yer think," he muttered to Constable Jones.

"Frightens yer more like it, makes you wonder."

"Wonder what?"

"Whether the Insurance Company will pay his

life assurance?"

"What?"

"Act of God, chuckled, Jones, "They usually wriggle out of them..."